Readers love *To the Highest Bidder* by CAITLIN RICCI

"This was a wonderfully written book."

—MM Good Book Reviews

"…a solid story with an interesting plot hook. I will admit, I found the brief epilogue emotionally rewarding, too."

—Joyfully Jay

"…her writing voice was so strong I truly felt compelled to read this one to the end."

—The Novel Approach

"…the storyline, the simple way the author explained the sci-fi elements… and the way she handled the ending was excellent…"

—Three Books Over the Rainbow

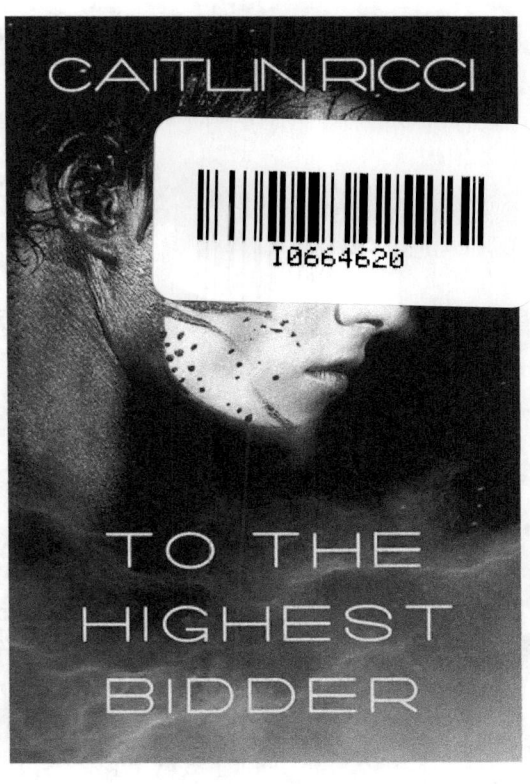

"This was my first Caitlin Ricci title, but I was not disappointed… I certainly look forward to picking up more from this author."

—Convergence Book Reviews

By CAITLIN RICCI

Blood Slave
Country Strong
Cuddling (Dreamspinner Anthology)
For the Asking
His Lion Tamer
Marked by Grief
One More Time
With Cari Z Worth the Wait

A FOREVER HOME
Rescuing Jack
Of Monsters and Men

A PLANET CALLED WISH
To the Highest Bidder
Fantasy for a Gentleman

Published by Harmony Ink Press
Crush
First Time for Everything (Harmony Ink Anthology)
Weathering the Storm

Published by DREAMSPINNER PRESS
www.dreamspinnerpress.com

FANTASY
FOR A
GENTLEMAN

CAITLIN RICCI

Published by
DREAMSPINNER PRESS

5032 Capital Circle SW, Suite 2, PMB# 279, Tallahassee, FL 32305-7886 USA
www.dreamspinnerpress.com

Fantasy for a Gentleman
© 2016 Caitlin Ricci.

Cover Art
© 2016 Caitlin Ricci.
Cover content is for illustrative purposes only and any person depicted on the cover is a model.

ISBN: 978-1-63476-869-6
Digital ISBN: 978-1-63476-870-2
Library of Congress Control Number: 2015918976
Published February 2016
v. 1.0

Printed in the United States of America
∞
This paper meets the requirements of
ANSI/NISO Z39.48-1992 (Permanence of Paper).

CHAPTER
ONE

I TOOK my time showering between clients, as I always did. It was as if I was refreshing myself, wiping away one personality and replacing it with another. The perfect one that would suit the next person who wanted to spend time with me. I appreciated each of them, and even adored some of them. It was because they kept coming back to visit me at Asiq that I could stay in the brothel and do what I enjoyed, which probably sounded strange to some people. I knew plenty well how my love of the job confused my little brother, Thierry. I wasn't sure how to explain it any better to him either. It wasn't that having sex with different people every day made me happy, but that was part of it.

For me the enjoyment of my job came from the idea that I could make people feel better, not simply in the moments they were with me, but overall. It wasn't a life my brother could understand, but it had been working out well for me over the last ten years.

Part of my happiness likely came from where I worked too. I hadn't applied to any other brothel on the pleasure planet of Wish, so I wasn't sure if my views of the life I led would have changed had I not always been at Asiq, but within the lavish walls, we aspasians were treated with kindness and respect. We weren't whores, as some likely considered us to be. We were entertainers, companions, and friends. I knew about my clients' children, their spouses, and all the other people in their lives who they considered special and important enough to talk to someone like me about.

Coming out of the bathroom with only a pair of low-slung black pants on, I waved to the small blinking camera, barely larger than my thumbnail, nestled in a corner of the small bookshelf. Monroe, the owner of Asiq and the man my little brother was in love with, could see the entire room from that point. And I knew he was watching. He always watched, always made sure we were safe while we were with our clients. I didn't mind that in the least.

I had about ten minutes until my next client was going to be there. Mr. Saunders was Nafsu, a person with gray skin and small bony nubs that ran over his arms and along the back of his head. He'd become much more of a regular after winning his senate seat, but our games never changed, and I knew to secure my wrists in the soft, easy-release ties. Before I did that, though, I slipped a blue cover over my eyes, blinding me. The ties I could handle by touch, and Senator Saunders had long ago told me his preferences. I wouldn't indulge some of them, especially the ones where he wanted to try out having my brother and me together at the same time, but having me tied up and apparently helpless was hardly something I would complain about. My clients all had their quirks, and his wasn't at all strange to me.

I heard the door to my room open, and I settled in on my knees. He said nothing to me, which was a little strange, since the senator was usually so chatty, but maybe he had something on his mind. He touched me on my shoulder, and I held still, letting him touch me where he wanted. I could always stop my sessions, and it wasn't as if I was being forced to do this at all, so where he got to touch me was where I allowed him.

Unsurprisingly he slid his hand from my shoulder, down my side, and to my stomach. I took care of myself, and my clients noticed the definition in my muscles and often commented on it. I was Sythe, though, the most reactive of any alien species known in the universe, and Senator Saunders hadn't come just to see me tied up. He'd come to watch me *feel*.

Tearing my nerves open and feeling myself heat up was a normal occurrence. I was always just below boiling, a barely restrained ball of desire and excited nerve endings. I sighed with pleasure as he slid his rough fingertips down my stomach, hesitating at the band of my pants, then going past until I felt them brush against my base.

I heard the door open again, and I turned my head toward the sound. Monroe would have told me if I was booked for a double session. "Corbin, move!"

I knew Monroe's voice and trusted him implicitly. The ties were easy to get off my wrists, and I rolled away from the senator. Only once I pulled the cover off my eyes, I saw that the man in front of me, the one who had been about to grab me, wasn't Senator Saunders. I crouched on the bed, very glad Monroe had come in when he had.

"Who are you?" I demanded.

He was Nafsu, but he was likely no older than my own forty-two, not the senator's sixty years or so. And he was built, even more so than I was. He hadn't removed any of his own clothing, but beneath the tight black shirt, I could see enough muscle that, if the situation hadn't been so out of place, I might have drooled.

"Don't waste time wondering who he is," Monroe said, raising a nonlethal neutralizing gun in his direction. But the man was faster and hit Monroe squarely in the chest with his own.

I didn't worry about Monroe because he was fine. Neutralizing guns were made to keep someone immobile and were good for peacekeepers. Monroe had one to protect us. I was more concerned with why the man in front of me, who wore no badge or official uniform, would have a gun like that. "What do you want with me?" I asked him. I flicked my gaze to the door, and he must have followed the movement of my eyes because he smiled at me.

"I've come to kill you, Corbin Leroux. I promise that I will make your death swift, but I do need to take your life."

I knew this would be a man without pity, and who, even if I could force myself to cry right then, wouldn't have been persuaded to spare my life. He might have been expecting someone meek, someone who would try to beg and plead. Instead he got me, and I was a bit tougher than most people gave me credit for.

3

He was close enough to the bed, within grabbing distance if I wanted to, so I launched myself and landed on him heavily. We struggled, and I kneed him as hard as I could in his groin, which distracted him into dropping the gun. It was an easy thing for me then to roll off him, pick up the gun, and point it at him.

Monroe mumbled something I couldn't understand as he came out of being immobilized. I didn't pay any attention to him, though, since I was too busy trying to figure out where to shoot my would-be murderer. "Why try to kill me?" I asked him.

"You've got a bounty on your head. Two thousand credits."

His answer surprised me, first because no one, to my knowledge, had ever wanted me dead before. But also because I should have been worth a whole lot more than that. "I make that number of credits in two sessions with my clients. If that. Who wants me dead for so little?"

He looked surprised at my question and might have even smiled at me before Monroe shot him with his gun. The expression died on my bounty hunter's face, and I relaxed my arm as I turned to see Monroe struggling to sit up as the pellet of neutralizing toxin naturally worked its way out of his bloodstream.

"You're lucky you're fast," he said with a cough as he rubbed at his chest.

I smirked and put the gun down on the bed behind me as I knelt down beside the bounty hunter. He was still alive, still very much awake, and I saw him move his eyes toward me. If he could show emotion right then, I wondered if he would look afraid. Or maybe he was just more curious than anything as I patted him down, looking for his identification holoscreen.

Bodies were normal for me. Everyone had one, and most people wanted me to touch theirs. When I was on Wish, it seemed like everyone either wanted to touch mine or wanted me to touch theirs. I took this for the compliment it was. So when I slid my hand into the front pocket of his pants and my fingers brushed up against his hard length before I curled my hand around his holoscreen, I should not have been embarrassed. I also should not have felt my nerves flare up uncontrollably. It had been less than an hour since I'd last had my needs taken care of. While it was normal for me to be able to find enjoyment many times a day, as a Sythe I felt as if I shouldn't have been quite so interested in a man who had, only a few minutes before, wanted to kill me.

"He's using a fake name," I said instantly, after I turned on the holoscreen and read over the letters.

Monroe held out his hand for the little black square, and I put it in his palm. "Nafsu don't use *y*'s in their names."

I'd caught that as well, and the man was trying to go by Brimley. "Silly tradition really, and not many people would have noticed it or that you only vaguely resemble the man in the stolen ID that you were carrying." Most people would have been too distracted by how good-looking he was. I slid my hand to the bounty hunter's throat and pressed my thumb a little against his windpipe in a threat. "You were so ready to kill me." I shook my head and released his neck. He may have been a killer, but I was certainly not.

"And now I'll take care of him." Monroe was strong enough to stand up, to get to his feet, and he shot the man again for good measure. I saw the pain in his eyes, though he couldn't move, and said nothing. He was lucky Monroe hadn't shot him in his dick for what he'd try to do to one of his aspasians.

"Will you spare him?"

Monroe only gave me a look, as if he couldn't believe I was stupid enough to ask such a ridiculous thing. "No."

"He didn't kill me," I reminded him.

"He tried to. Why in the universe would you want him to live?" Monroe practically snapped at me.

I didn't have a good answer to his question. But I still didn't want the bounty hunter to die. "Let him go. If he tries again, I'll kill him myself."

Monroe couldn't argue with me, not really. If he killed the bounty hunter, most people would have forgiven him. But as far as the law of the system went, the bounty hunter hadn't been trying to use a lethal weapon on me. Maybe after I'd been immobilized he would have killed me, but it made more sense, to me at least, to kill the person that you'd been paid to and not simply for him to make me unable to fight back. Except....

"Hey, you." I lightly slapped the back of my hand against his cheek, which got me his attention as he turned a pair of icy-blue eyes toward me. "Look down if you were going to try to screw me after I wasn't able to fight you. Look up if you were going to just drag me out and kill me somewhere else or something equally mundane but that I'd still have clothes on for."

He looked up instantly, and I met Monroe's worried gaze. "If he'd looked down I would have let you kill him."

"I should have let him kill you for your stupidity."

I laughed and got off the floor. "Maybe. But I make you too many credits." I patted Monroe on his shoulder then jumped on the bed. My time had been booked up for the hour, and since I wasn't having sex during it, I was going to take a nap until my next client came to see me. "Night."

"You aren't even going to help me carry him outside?" Monroe asked me as if he couldn't believe my nerve. After years of working for him and having him be in love with my brother and willing to do anything for Thierry, I'd put myself in a position where I could get away with more than anyone else in Asiq. "Get off your ass, and help me here, Corbin," Monroe gruffly snapped at me, and I knew better than to push him. Even I couldn't get away with everything.

I helped drag the bounty hunter out, and we left him lying in one of Wish's many alleys. He wouldn't be able to get back into Asiq, not without one of us giving him permission, since everyone was scanned when they walked through the front doors. I was pretty sure I was safe because of that standard security measure, and when my next client came in shortly after I returned to my room, I was ready for them.

Sex was easy, uncomplicated, and simple. Giving pleasure was a wonderful experience for me, and I was sure I would have enjoyed seeing the people I was with being passionate even if I wasn't an aspasian or Sythe. Molding myself to the body of my client, my momentary lover, I became part of them. I was whoever they wanted me to be, and I answered to whatever name they wanted to call me.

I loved my life, and for a little while, when they were with me, I gave them everything I had and loved them too.

CHAPTER
TWO

I WAS on my home station a week later with my shuttle docked outside my living room and my butt planted on the low couch as I started to relax. Wish was a four-hour ride away from my home, so I should have been relaxed after such a long flight, but I never seemed to completely unwind until I was back home.

I had my eyes closed and was very nearly asleep when someone overrode my security measures and popped open the airlock between the shuttle bay and my front door. I got up quickly, ready to defend myself if I needed to even though I didn't have anything but my fists to do so with, and waited for the intruder to reveal themselves.

As strange as it was, it took me a second to figure out I was supposed to be afraid as the bounty hunter stepped through my front door, once again wearing all black like that was some sort of unspoken uniform for his profession. Maybe it was. I didn't have all that much experience with bounty hunters as a general rule unless they were clients, and I couldn't remember if any of the people I spent time with had divulged that particular detail about themselves.

"Are we doing this again?" I asked him, gathering nerve from somewhere. He nodded and raised his neutralizing gun in my direction. I was running toward my bedroom before he'd pulled the trigger the first time, narrowly missing me.

"I am sorry that I will be forced to kill you. This isn't personal on my end, you are simply a mark, a job, and I want to be paid," he called out to me as I locked myself in the room.

8

Neutralizing guns were useless against anything that wasn't a living, breathing thing, so at least he couldn't use it to get into my room. But apparently he wasn't above trying to kick my door down as I shook harder with each loud bang.

"You may want to be paid, but I'd rather live!" I shouted back at him over the sound of him trying to break into my bedroom. I should have just let Monroe kill him.

Still, I wasn't scared. I didn't question what he would do to me if he could, and I had no intention of dying that day, but I wasn't afraid of him, which was incredibly stupid. The sounds of him trying to get into my room eventually slowed, but I knew he was still there. Being an aspasian, I'd gotten used to figuring out where people were near me. It helped me react to them when I was blindfolded, and running into the other guys while we danced on stage together for the entertainment of the guests in Asiq was hardly sexy.

"I'll triple what you're being paid," I said, hoping he could hear me since I didn't want to start shouting through the walls. It wouldn't really be all that hard to do. Six thousand credits wasn't much.

"Let me in, and we can talk."

"Or you could try to kill me again," I said with a snicker. I must have been crazy to want to laugh at him for wanting me dead. He had no reason to, no one did. I had no enemies, no one who wanted me dead. That I knew of. Apparently I was wrong, though, because someone had hired a Nafsu to do just that. It was so strange, so out of the usual for my life, that I wasn't sure how to react, how I was supposed to feel about it. I thought I was supposed to be afraid, but I couldn't bring myself to be. He was big and probably scary to some people. But not to me. I only wanted to know who he was working for, and what had made them decide that I was supposed to die.

"I give you my word that I won't try to kill you should you let me in," he said. And, stupid me, I kind of believed him. It was something in his voice, in the way he sounded so sincere as he promised not to kill me. This whole situation was simply too ridiculous. I opened the door before I could think better of it, and the first thing I noticed was

9

his surprise, as if he couldn't believe I'd done that. Really, I couldn't either. He lowered his gun while I stood there watching him.

"Tell me who wants to kill me," I demanded.

"Senator Saunders," he told me, as if he had no code of secrecy. I could hardly remember a time when I hadn't lived by that code, so hearing the information given to me so easily made me cautious, especially when the name of the person who wanted me dead really started to sink in.

"Why does he want to kill me?"

The bounty hunter shrugged. "I'm not given that information. Only a price and a target."

Fair enough. "What's your name? Your real name this time."

"Emmanuel Leoniste," he answered me, the seriousness of his voice telling me it was the truth that he spoke. It was a nice name, and it suited him somehow. Gentle, but with an underlying strength that I already knew not to mess with. I did smile at him, though, relaxing with him despite the situation.

"I'd like to say it's nice to meet you, only I'm not sure it is, given how interested you seem to be in killing me."

"You're nothing more than a stack of credits for me."

"That's comforting. At least you wanting to kill me isn't personal."

He smiled at me and gave me the slightest nod. "It's never personal with any of my targets. If I didn't try to kill you, someone else would come for you. He wants you dead."

I had an idea, but it sounded completely ridiculous in my head, and even worse coming out of my mouth. "How much would you need to not kill me? And to keep other bounty hunters from killing me?" I knew how much I made on average, and it was good money. I also wasn't above offering myself if that meant I got to live awhile longer without looking over my shoulder for someone carrying a neutralizing gun all the time.

Emmanuel put his gun away and crossed his arms over his chest as if considering my offer. "Six thousand credits up front, two thousand a month after that."

Six would be most of my savings, but I could easily replenish my accounts the next time I was on Wish. "For how long?"

"Until the senator grows tired of losing his best bounty hunters mysteriously, I'd imagine."

Which could take years, but I was willing to pay that. He was merciless, which I supposed I needed, in a way. This was such new territory for me that I might have been making the wrong decision each step of the way and not even know about it until it was too late. Which would mean that I would be dead.

I was about to agree to his demands when he tacked on another one. "And weekly visits while you are in Asiq. To discuss the measures I've taken to ensure your continued survival."

I highly doubted his motives for wanting to see me weekly when I was at work; after all, he had tried to put his hand down the front of my pants, but we were working out a bargain, and I didn't find him unattractive. Despite his willingness to kill me, and others.

"Deal. I will transfer the first sum of credits to an account of your choosing immediately. Now, tell me why the senator wants me dead." That was my next concern, since, to my knowledge, I'd never done anything to warrant that kind of anger. But apparently I had somehow.

"Can we sit first?" he asked me, and my manners—and training as an aspasian—kicked in.

"Sure." It was almost nice, in a way, to see this man for who he was—someone who only wanted to get paid—and not as someone who lurked in the shadows waiting to jump out at me. The monster I knew and all that, as the Old Earth saying went.

I made him a fruit-caffeine-foam mixture from the small machine in the kitchen, then brought it over to him. I only wanted water. We sat on opposite sides of the living room, staring at each other until I turned away. If he was going to kill me, then he was going to have to try a lot harder than he had been. I wouldn't go down easily. He lacked honor, but if he had been loyal to Senator Saunders, I would still be fighting him for my life, so I didn't fault him for that one personality flaw at all.

"The senator received a message from someone willing to blackmail him. Clearly, by the secrets they knew, it was one of his whores. But they masked their voice, and the senator decided to send us out, one for each of the whores—"

I had to stop him there. "Aspasian. They may have been whores, but I'm an aspasian. Show some respect."

"No," he said, snickering.

I rolled my eyes. "Do you even know the difference?"

Emmanuel looked bored. "I have no reason to. I don't visit your kind."

"A whore can make you come, an aspasian can make you feel loved, wanted, as if for that hour or two you're all that exists in their world," I explained, even though I doubted that it would change anything in his mind. I was proud of what I did and who I was. It made me mad that he apparently couldn't be bothered to care about even that most basic difference.

He sat back and brought one of his legs over the other. "I don't believe you. Show me."

I wasn't that stupid. Not by a long shot. "No. I'm not working at the moment. Will you leave now?"

Emmanuel smiled at me. "Ready to throw me out?"

I was ready the moment he had broken into my apartment. "Yes."

"Then pay me." He handled me a holoscreen with an account number on it. I took mine out as well and transferred the credits to him.

"Done," I said, putting mine back away. He took his from me as well.

Getting up, he smoothed out his black pants and straightened his jacket. "When are you next in Asiq?"

"Two weeks," I replied, watching him head toward the front door.

"Then that's when I'll see you again."

Waving to him, I was glad to see him quietly go. The next person I talked to would not be so calm. I knew that and braced myself for Monroe's anger even as I put the earpiece in my ear and started up the comcall on my wrist.

"Miss me?" Monroe asked, answering the phone.

I wished I was calling for something that simple. Monroe was a friend, and I'd called him often simply to talk, especially after he'd fallen in love with my brother. Monroe was practically family now as far as I was concerned, though I did still try to keep some professionalism in our relationship while I was at work. "No. The bounty hunter from Asiq came by and—"

"You'll come back to Asiq immediately, and I'll put you under protection." He was all business in just those few seconds between his first words and the next ones.

He really didn't have to go to those extremes. I didn't see the situation as being that dire. Not even a little. "He and I worked it out, but he will be visiting me there. So I need you to let him in. Please."

"You expect me to open my doors to someone who tried to kill one of my employees? Have you lost your mind somewhere in that station you live on?"

Probably. "We have a deal." I didn't want to tell him the details, largely because I didn't want him trying to interfere and finding a solution on his own. The deal worked for me, and I could easily afford it. I saw no reason for Monroe to know the particulars about it. He took good care of us all already, my brother and me especially. I didn't need more from him now.

"Can he be trusted?"

That, I didn't know. "As much as any bounty hunter can be I suppose. He doesn't seem crazy, if that's what you mean."

"I don't like it."

Of course he didn't. There was no good reason to like this plan, because it was ridiculous. But it was the best one I had. The only one I had, actually, that didn't involve me dying. So it was the one I would be going with. But I needed Monroe to agree, since Asiq was his.

"I don't either, but I'd like to live."

He gave me a harsh, dry laugh in response, and even though there was no happiness in the sound, it still made me smile. He was a good friend, and I knew by his laughter that he was going to agree with me, even before he spoke. "Here are my terms. First, this trouble can never affect your brother. I don't care what you have to tell him as long as it isn't anything about you having a client that is a bounty hunter intent on killing you. He has enough to focus on."

It was good to know that Monroe was still in love with my brother, even eight years after they first got together. It hadn't been the traditional way of meeting someone, but, then again, so very few things in our lives ever seemed to be. I was a Sythe orphan, and I'd spent most of my life taking care of my little brother. Thierry had sold his virginity to Monroe, and somehow they'd fallen in love. I didn't need, or want, the details. But even though I understood it had been years since they'd seen each other, I could hear how much Thierry loved him every time we spoke. It was heartwarming, and if I was jealous that my brother had found someone who loved him for exactly who he was, then I tried not to let that show.

"Anything else you want me to agree to? Because that one is easy," I said as I got up to run the cup Emmanuel had used through the chemical sanitizer. Water was better and didn't leave a metallic aftertaste, but water was in perpetual shortage on the station. I couldn't wait to have a glass of real ice water back in Asiq, where Monroe spared no expense when it came to taking care of his clients, or us.

"Yes, when he's there, you will let me know. If I believe that you're in danger in any way, I will come in."

"Of course." That was standard protocol. Sometimes clients went further than what we were expecting. I knew when to call in reinforcements, though I hadn't had an incident in years. People that simply wanted someone to smack around for a while generally couldn't afford me.

"Good. I don't want to be the one to tell your brother that you were a fool and got yourself killed."

His words made me laugh. "Not sure of that, maybe you would simply rather not lose that many credits each month."

"This is true. Stay alive for the next two weeks, and I'll see you back in Asiq."

"Will do." I ended the comcall and pulled the earpiece out of my ear, giving it a tug. The little bud was sometimes very uncomfortable, leaving the inside of my ear red and tender.

After sitting down on my couch again, I leaned my head back and closed my eyes, intent on relaxing for the next two weeks until I went back to the job I loved and the clients who loved me, along with one new client, one that I wished I wasn't so curious about.

CHAPTER THREE

WISH WAS a vibrant planet full of artificial sunlight to complement the natural sun; a planet constantly bathed in light, where every color imaginable was on display in vivid silks and sheer curtains hanging from the windows of the brothels. In the harsher parts of Wish, whores worked long hours for little pay and dealt with horrible clients. So close to the landing ports, the brothels gave way to markets, all except for one.

Asiq stood in a prime location, situated between two markets, and was the first, and only, brothel people coming to the planet saw. I stopped and grabbed some lick fruit from a market stall, biting into it instantly and feeling the fruit pop on my tongue as the seeds exploded with the contact of foreign matter. They were a fun treat, a hybrid only sold on Wish because of an exclusive contract. They were something Monroe didn't like us to have when we were about to see clients because, after the fruit was gone, our tongues tended to be a bit sensitive with all the little explosions going off.

Lucky me, as a Sythe, I was already sensitive, so it hardly bothered me. And I always had a few hours in between landing and when I saw my first client anyway. At only four hours, my trip was shorter than most of the men I worked with, which meant I was able to relax and get back into the kind of life Asiq let me lead, instead of needing to nap in my room for those few hours. I came in, got my handprint scanned, then headed into my room. Number twelve was mine for the next two weeks. That was always my number.

I put my bag, filled with my clothes, in the closet and tossed the fruit into the waste system port in the side wall. Next up were the test and vaccine, standard procedure each time we came back to Asiq. There was a shiny black panel in the wall, standing out in sharp contrast to the pale green walls of my room, and I went to it, stripping off my shirt as I walked.

"Name?" the mechanical voice asked me as I touched the panel.

"Corbin Leroux." The thumbprint oval lit up, and I pressed my right thumb to that spot. The panel beeped, and the cover slid away, revealing the two devices I would need. After so many years on Wish, this was so second nature to me that I hardly even thought about the fine prick of the needles as they bit into my skin, taking my blood for the test. I put the device back into the hole behind the panel where the device would read the test, send the data wirelessly to Monroe, and self-clean for the next person who used my room. I didn't know who they were, as I only socialized with the guys on my shift, and there was always a solid twelve hours between shifts in which Asiq was closed for cleaning every two weeks.

The vaccine, in general, hurt. Sometimes I could distract myself thinking about something else, but more often than not, like today, it made me grit my teeth together until finally it was done and I could breathe again. I put that cylinder into the hole as well, and the panel closed as soon as my fingers were clear. My shoulder, where I'd pressed the vaccine in, was still a bit sore, but I expected that. And I was fine with that little bit of pain. It was part of working at Asiq, a brothel that only served the best clientele and where I felt safe working.

My com lit up on my wrist as I started heading toward the bowl of chocolates that was in every room of the brothel, just waiting to be consumed by us greedy little aspasians and our clients. "Hello?" I answered the call, putting the earpiece I always had on me into my ear.

"Your first client says his name is Emmanuel and that you'd know who he is."

Good old Monroe, right to business. "That would be the bounty hunter. Is he here already?"

"He is. Are you accepting clients this early, or do you want him to come back in a few hours after you've had a chance to rest?"

"Send him in." We wouldn't be having sex, so I figured I could rest and talk to him at the same time.

"Okay."

There was no judgment in Monroe's voice, only the silence at the end of the call, and I waited for the knock on my door, which came a few minutes later. "Come in." I didn't get up. This was business, even more so than what I normally did, and since I wasn't there to entertain him in any way, I felt no need to put on a show for him either.

He wore black, again, and I wondered if the color was all he owned. Today, though, he had on a tight-fitting jacket with small silver buckles at the cuffs over yet another pair of black pants. I saw a gun hanging from each of his hips, and I focused on them, before raising my gaze to his, letting him know that I saw he was armed. And that I wasn't afraid.

He smirked and closed the door behind himself. "How does this go, then?"

I put my hands behind my head and watched him. He hadn't asked me to be his fantasy, so I was only me. Lazy, completely relaxed me. Who didn't have the time or the inclination to play games with him. "Well… if you were a client, I wouldn't be just lying here. Unless we'd talked about that beforehand and I knew you wanted me like this."

"As the senator wanted you with your wrists tied and a blindfold over your eyes?" he asked me.

Normally talking about my clients with another client would be a horrible breach of confidentiality. Except in this circumstance, where all my usual rules seemed to have been thrown out the airlock. "Yes," I said, still hesitant. This was one of the first rules Monroe had instilled in me, and even though I knew this was different, it still felt strange to say.

"Do you play those games with any of your other clients?"

There was the line, and it was a strict one. "I'm not telling."

He took a few steps closer to me and sat down at the foot of the bed, close to me but not nearly as close as my usual clients would be. Though I did have one man who just wanted to hear me talk to him as he stood on the other side of the room from me. I catered to all types as long as they didn't hurt me in some way.

"Did you know that bounty hunters are able to torture their targets? We're outside of the law of any system's government."

I rolled my eyes. "And the information you'd torture me for is which of my clients has a bit of a kink?" There was some merit in that thought, since many high-profile men came to visit me regularly, and I remembered everything about each of them. Before he could consider that plan, I sat up then went to my knees, crawling toward him on the bed in the sexiest way I knew how. "How about we find out what kind of games you like to play instead?" I ran my hand down his arm, starting at his shoulder, and he pulled away from me before I could get to his elbow.

Nafsu didn't blush, not really. Their skin was so gray any hint of color was barely noticeable unless, like me, a person was looking for it. And I saw it there, the lightest brush of pink against his high gray cheekbones. Then there was the slightest tick in his jaw, the last sign I needed to know that I got to him. He may have been the one who was armed, but I wasn't powerless. Not when I so clearly affected him as much as I did.

"I'll be back to see you in a few weeks."

Frowning, I sat back on my heels. "You just got here. Didn't you want to talk or something?"

He hesitated, as if I'd reminded him that he hadn't come to Wish only to see me, but he still left me kneeling there on my bed, with the quiet closing of my door. I smirked and lay back down. It was just as well, probably. Only, maybe he wasn't done with me so quickly, as I heard a knock on my door, which I quickly got up to answer.

"Yes?" I said, looking at him as he stood in the hallway. I remembered my manners and Monroe's rules a second later—that clients were never to linger in the hallway—as I grabbed him by the front of his jacket and pulled him inside the room.

Once I had the door closed behind him, I went back to the bed and sat down with my legs crossed, waiting for him to say something.

"I spoke to the senator this week, I thought you should know," he began.

I nodded, that would be information I'd like to have. "And what did he say?"

Emmanuel looked at me seriously, as if I wasn't going to like the answer. "My peers have collected the bounty on four of your... the other people he visited, like he did with you."

"Were they all on Wish?"

He shook his head and joined me on the bed, looking stiff and uncomfortable on the overly plush mattress that had been designed for ultimate comfort in mind. "No, only one was. And she was on the other side of the planet."

I felt badly for her, but part of me thought that it was better her than me. At least I was still alive, and I intended to stay that way. "How long did you have to kill me?"

"Thirty days, which are already up."

Frowning, I sighed. "Will he send another after me, then? Since you couldn't kill me?"

"Wouldn't, not couldn't. I could kill you anytime I wanted to."

That made me roll my eyes. However he wanted to put it, that was fine. As long as he answered my question. "Well?"

He moved his fingers to the back of my hand, and since his expression didn't change, I wondered if he noticed what he was doing at all. "More may come for you, but we let each other know when we are close to one another so that we don't accidently poach a target. I'll know that they are here before they kill you."

As reassuring as that was, I didn't feel all that much safer. "And if they come in as a client and happen to recognize me? What's your plan, then?"

He circled his fingers around my wrist, and I shut my nerves down tightly. I wasn't nearly as good at shutting them down as my brother was, since I was so used to being open all the time both to get potential clients to notice me and current clients to be happy with me, but I was able to do it a little. I could have pulled my hand away, though, which would have been simpler, but I didn't want him to stop touching me. I liked the contact too much.

"You'd be on your own, then. Do you have any limits on what can happen during your time with the men you whore with?" he asked.

Now I did pull away from him. "I'm an aspasian. My life here is more than sex and sucking dicks. Try to remember that if you want this deal to continue between us. I may not want to die tomorrow, but that doesn't mean that I'll put up with being insulted whenever you happen to come around either." He'd offended me, and I was quick to get off the bed and put some space between us.

"Then what is it that you do?"

I yanked back on my anger a little and considered what he was actually saying. He didn't know because he'd never been around one of us before. "How many brothels have you been to?"

There was definite color in his cheeks now. "None."

"But you have been with someone before, haven't you?" I pressed. The gender of the other person, or people as was likely the case, given that he looked to be about the same age as me, didn't matter at all. I only wanted to make sure I wasn't dealing with a nervous virgin here. I was too much for most of them, and I didn't exactly have a way to pull back who I was in order to make them more comfortable. I was Sythe, and we made excellent lovers because we held nothing back. It could be overwhelming for people who weren't used to us, to say the least.

He looked at me as if I had lost my mind, and I was instantly relieved. Not a virgin, then. "Of course I have."

There was no "of course" about it. I'd met some people in my time in Asiq—some of my best clients actually—that had absolutely no interest in sex. They only wanted company, possibly to be held, and sometimes danced with. I didn't tell him any of that, though. All he needed to know was that my life on Asiq was so much more than what he thought I did in my time here.

"Most of the time I'm not naked when I'm working here," I began to explain. "People are a complicated mix of what they want, what they need, and what turns them on. Some don't even want anything sexual. There are plenty of people who come here simply for the conversation or for whatever else they want from me."

I had a lady who told me I reminded her of her son who had passed long before she'd met me. She'd been coming to me for years, sharing her memories of him and simply having someone to talk to. I looked forward to seeing her each month, and I considered her a friend. Maybe, in time, Emmanuel would be one of my clients-turned-friends too. As long as he didn't try to kill me again. That thought had me smiling.

"Do you have a list of what you do, then?" he asked.

I came back to the bed and sat down beside him again so we could talk civilly, like men ought to do. "Like a menu? No. I'm not an eatery. You tell me what you want, and if I don't do that, or don't know how to, then I refer to you to someone in Asiq who does. What are you looking for?"

"Do you kiss?"

I had to bite back hard on my laugh. "Yes. I certainly do kiss my clients, when they want me to. Is that what you want?"

He was quick to shake his head, and I tried not to let my impatience show. I wasn't used to someone being so indecisive with me, as I'd been with most of my clients for at least a few months, and together we had figured out exactly what they wanted, and expected, from me. Even in the beginning sessions, none of my clients were this absolutely shy around me, as if they couldn't even bear to look at me. Where had the man who wanted to kill me gone? I wanted him back. He, at least, made sense to me.

Moving as slowly as I possibly could, to the point of hardly feeling like I was moving at all, I eventually got my hand on his shoulder. He looked at me as if I had suddenly become the predator and he was my prey. It was an interesting change of pace from how we'd been during our last interaction.

I leaned in closer to him and added my mouth to where my hand had been, kissing his shoulder, then across to his back, and then his neck.

"Enough. I don't want you kissing me." His voice had grown cold, and I moved away instantly.

"Fine."

He turned to look at me, and I was surprised at the amount of disgust in his expression. My actions, and my life, didn't warrant that kind of an expression from him. "You don't have any room to give me that for my job. You kill people for credits."

"There is honor in what I do," he retorted angrily.

I bit back my sarcastic laughter. "Honor? You only care about money. There's no honor in that."

"And you play games with the hearts of men."

His words genuinely confused me. "I care about everyone who comes into this room, no matter who they are or what they want from me. So what game is it that you think I'm playing?"

"The one where you pretend to be interested," he snapped.

Ah. So that was what his problem was. I tried not to roll my eyes and failed. "You want to see how I feel when you're nearby? You'd have to touch me for that."

Emmanuel frowned at me, but he did come closer. He stopped before he was close enough for me to touch, hovering just outside my reach. I was a patient man, and one not prone to easily giving up, so I waited for him to make up his mind. Either he would let me touch him, let me kiss him, or he wouldn't.

Either way, I was safe there in Asiq, and our arrangement would be intact for another few weeks. He surprised me by grabbing me roughly by my long hair that hung nearly down to my butt, twisting it around his hand, and controlling where I went. I grinned, not minding this game at all. I expected him to kiss me, to control me and be rough with me in that moment as well.

Only he didn't. Instead he simply held my hair in his fist, making me wait for him to act. He didn't hurt me, and I knew plenty well how to defend myself if he had tried. But he didn't. I waited, looking into his blue eyes and expecting him to be angry with me, only he looked simply curious, as if I was a puzzle he couldn't figure out. I couldn't even tell if he wanted to try or not. I had sex with people because that was my job, and if he wanted to, I would have been with him too, but I was curious about him because of how he was. He was strange to me, in that I wasn't used to people who didn't instantly know what they wanted to do with me. Even when I met with new clients, they always had this fantasy in their heads, usually of something they felt uncomfortable telling anyone but someone like me. I was an aspasian; fulfilling fantasies was my business.

However, I had no idea what his was, especially as he released my hair from around his wrist and simply began stroking his fingers through the strands. I watched Emmanuel as he continued to play with the ends of my hair, running my black strands through his fingers. To me, he was a snake waiting to strike. And part of me wanted him to, because then I would know what to expect from him. Right now, outside of not killing me, I didn't know anything else about his plan.

"How many men have you killed?" I asked him idly.

He gave me a soft, secret smile. "How many have you been with?" His expression was a mystery to me as it turned dangerous, nearly hard, though his smile stayed in place. And yet, he continued playing with the ends of my hair.

"Hundreds," I answered him honestly. He stopped his hand on my hair and stared at me for a long moment. "You?"

"Would it frighten you to know that number?"

Very little frightened me, especially when it came to Emmanuel. I shook my head, earning myself a smile, and, a moment later, the softest kiss I'd ever experienced as he brought his lips forward to meet mine.

I responded, as I did to every kiss a client ever gave me, and opened my mouth for him just as I flayed my nerves apart, reacting to him on the deepest level that I could. He brought his hand to the

24

side of my hip, and I felt sparks of electricity fly across my skin. This was why people loved being with us: we Sythe experienced physical pleasure much more deeply than anyone else in the universe as far as I knew, and it was impossible for us not to share that with the people we were with.

He started to lift up my shirt, and I pulled our hips together. My com beeped a second later, two low, barely audible sounds that would hardly draw the attention of my clients. But after years being in Asiq, I knew to pay attention to that sound.

"Time's up," I said reluctantly, meaning every bit of the feeling behind those words. I wanted him to stay. I wanted to see what he'd do once he had my shirt off, how far he'd let me go. But I had a tight schedule, and his session with me was over.

Emmanuel didn't try to argue with me, which was strange, but also a bit refreshing. Few people accepted that their time with me was over without at least a little begging. But he only nodded, stepping back and putting a good three feet between us. "I'll be back in a few weeks, then."

I'd still be right where he expected me to be. He headed to the door, didn't look back at me, and closed it tightly behind himself. As for me, I flopped back onto the bed, wondering what I was supposed to do with a budding attraction to a bounty hunter who would surely kill me as easily as he would join me in bed.

CHAPTER FOUR

I DIDN'T expect to see Emmanuel sitting there in my living room after I'd docked and come through the airlock two weeks later.

"I killed someone defending you last night. Another bounty hunter who was sent to finish the job I didn't," he said as soon as our eyes met.

It wasn't the way I would have started a conversation. But, then again, I had some manners and a bit of decorum when it came to dealing with other people. "Should I congratulate you?" I asked him as I walked around where he was sitting on my couch and went into my bedroom to put my bag down on the bed.

"A bit of thanks would be nice. I kept up my end of our bargain."

Rolling my eyes, I came back out and got a bit of juice to drink. Being the polite person I tried to be, I turned to offer him one, until I saw he'd already poured a drink for himself as if he somehow belonged in my apartment and had full access to everything in it. And, by the way he was watching me, maybe he thought that extended to myself as well. I didn't come near him to drink my juice, instead choosing to lean against the steel counter in the little space that passed for a kitchen on the station.

"I took a shot in the process."

If he was expecting pity from me, he was sorely mistaken. I didn't play that game when I was off work. "I'm sure it wasn't the first time. And you seem to be fairly alive still." My juice gone, I steamed the glass and left it there in the kitchen as I made my way toward him. After a moment of indecision, I decided to sit next to him on the couch. It was the most comfortable seat in the apartment, and just because he was there, I saw no reason to be uncomfortable.

He turned his head and leaned in for a kiss, which I quickly stopped with my palm pressed firmly against his lips. "What do you think you're doing?" I demanded.

Emmanuel pulled away, looking bewildered. "I was going to kiss you."

"I could figure that out for myself, thanks. My question is why you were," I said as I lowered my hand.

He frowned at me, and I waited for him to come up with something even halfway intelligent to say. "You didn't have a problem with it back on Wish."

If that was the best he could come up with, he had a lot to learn about spending time with aspasians like me. "That was back in Asiq. It doesn't translate to here. I don't let clients kiss me when I'm at home." Also, none of them knew where I lived. They weren't supposed to, and so I never saw them outside Asiq. I was different there. I was an aspasian, full of class and a desire to please my clients. Back home I was still polite, but I didn't have to be that person here, and I didn't talk to my clients when I was off Wish.

Here I was just me, simply Corbin, and I could be lazy and gross all I wanted to. I didn't have to shower, though I always did, and I didn't have to eat well, but I ate what I could afford to.

"What if I wasn't a client?"

I stared at him long and hard. "You aren't really a client anyway. You're someone I'm paying to keep the other bounty hunters off my back and not kill me at the same time, until Senator Saunders gets over wanting me killed."

He gave me a slow nod. "What if, though, I wanted more?" He reached for me, and I was quick to get off the couch and put as much distance between us as possible.

"I don't. At all."

Emmanuel looked hurt, then angry, as he got up and headed out of my apartment. He left through the station door, and I could hear him stomping up to the steel catwalk. My door locked automatically

Caitlin Ricci

as it closed. I released my breath and shook my head. Some clients were crazy. I'd met my fair share, but none of them knew where to find me once I left Asiq.

I wasn't exactly afraid of him, not really anyway. I knew he had the potential to hurt or even kill me, the gun that was an ever-present constant on his hip was proof enough of that, but I couldn't bring myself to be afraid of him. Still… it might be a good idea for me to lay low for a while, in case Emmanuel wanted to come back and argue with me or something like that. Really, I didn't know what he would do. After having him leave at Asiq, I hadn't thought he would want anything, so all of it was a surprise to me.

I put my earpiece in my ear and tried to think up a good lie while I waited for Monroe to answer my call.

"Hello, Corbin."

He sounded especially cheerful, and I was instantly suspicious. "Did you just get off a call with my brother?"

Monroe laughed. "I did. He says hello, in case you were wondering. He misses you. What did you want to call me about, though?"

"Can I come back to Asiq?"

"You just went home this morning," Monroe reminded me. He no longer sounded joyful; instead I only heard suspicion in his voice.

Finding a good lie was quickly failing me, and besides, if there was one thing Monroe valued more than credits, it was honesty from the people who worked for him. "The bounty hunter gave me a bit of trouble here. Nothing scary or violent, but I had to send him away. I was hoping I could come work for the next four weeks until my next normally scheduled break."

"I don't see why you couldn't, as long as you don't start slacking in any way. I'll expect you here by tomorrow morning, and a room will be made up for you. One of my regularly scheduled aspasians was a no-show today, so you can take his place for the next two weeks. Though, Corbin, is this bounty hunter someone that needs to be handled?"

28

I had to smile. "No. I'm fine, really. I just want to be back there, where my life and relationships make sense and where everyone has the same expectations of me. I'm a great aspasian. It's the part about being a man that I find complicated."

The humor was back in Monroe's voice as he laughed at what I'd said. "Yes, well, I believe you'll find many of the men that I employ completely the opposite of you. Perhaps you've been working here too long, and it has skewed your way of thinking."

His words were like a cold fist around my stomach. "Don't fire me. Please. You can't."

"I can, and will, do whatever I want, Corbin. Make no mistake about that. I will always do what's best for Asiq, and myself, and now your brother. You can rest easily, though, knowing that you are my best aspasian and even if your brother wasn't the man that I love, I would still think twice before kicking you out of Asiq. Now, I'm busy, you have things to do to prepare for coming back here. I will see you soon."

"Of course. Thank you, Monroe." He hung up before I'd finished talking.

I wasted no time in getting back to Asiq, arriving there only six hours later. I'd showered at home, had something to eat, then got back in my shuttle. Thankfully I budgeted well enough to be able to have the quick charge set up, along with the fuel, so that my shuttle was completely ready to go when I needed it and not the ten hours later that most shuttles at the station required. I liked having my freedom that way.

I didn't intend to go home for the next month and hadn't had a chance to clean the clothes I had brought back with me, so I knew I'd have to do laundry fairly soon after arriving at Asiq. Coming in through the back door, where we were supposed to enter so that the customers didn't see us before we were ready, I made my way straight to Monroe's office.

I knocked. I waited. I knocked again. I could hear him on a call with someone, and he was laughing. In all the years I'd known Monroe, I'd only heard him that happy while he was talking to Thierry.

I heard the nearly silent click of the door unlocking and let myself into his office, where he waved me in though he was still on the call.

"Your brother is here. … No, nothing's wrong. … I will talk to you later," Monroe said, and a few seconds later, he ended the comcall.

I was glad that they were together, but I couldn't say I especially liked the deception Monroe had pulled while my brother had been falling in love with him. But that was neither here nor there. Thierry was over it, and so was I.

"Where am I staying during this rotation?" I asked him.

He gave me a wide smile and leaned forward. He was careful not to touch me, not because there was some unspoken rule about him and his employees, but because I was so reactive. Thierry knew how to control his nerves. I wasn't nearly as good at it since I had to be open all the time while I was at work.

"Right down to business. I always did like that about you."

I nodded and waited for my room assignment.

"You'll be in twenty-six for the next two weeks. After that, you'll be back in twelve. I've never let anyone stay for a full six weeks. Don't burn yourself out. I'll start you off slowly, just in case you do need some time to rest up."

I smirked. Some of the other guys may have needed that kind of consideration, but I didn't. "You know most of my clients don't use me like that. I don't need you to go easy on me. If I need a break, I'll let you know before it starts affecting my work. But don't start me out slow just because you think I'm going to crash and burn. I can handle this, and I want to work."

Monroe nodded, but he didn't look away from me. "I'll give you a normal workload, for a week, then we will reassess. You haven't met any of these men, and I don't want them to think you're getting special treatment, so tell them you missed your last rotation and are filling in on this one."

"Easy enough. Will you have trouble booking me outside of my normal weeks?"

"There will never be a shortage of people wanting to spend time with a Sythe." He looked as if the words might have pained

30

him to say, as if he was trying very hard not to think of my brother at that moment. I knew Thierry was loyal to him, in love with him, and would have never strayed. But my brother had been out of the system for years now, and so I understood Monroe's uneasiness when it came to this matter.

I also knew that I didn't want to have anything to do with that kind of conversation. Monroe was my boss, and even though we were friendly, I tried very hard not to cross the boundary into friends. Maybe when Thierry came back that would change, but right now I liked to have everyone in their places. It left my life uncomplicated, simple, and completely organized. Just how I liked it.

"If the bounty hunter comes to visit me, will you let him?" I asked Monroe as I got to my feet. With my room assignment in place, I could begin working immediately once my test results were handed over to him and the vaccine was in my bloodstream. I was anxious to begin taking clients.

Monroe tilted his chin to the side. "Would you like to see him?"

"If he has the credits to pay for my time, I don't see why I shouldn't. He unnerved me, but I don't feel threatened by him," I replied with a shrug.

"Then I will let him in. Go on now. You know what to do."

I smirked at Monroe and did exactly that.

My first client of the night came no more than an hour later. I hadn't thought Monroe would be able to book me so quickly, but apparently he wasted no time in getting his credits. I didn't know the man who came to my door, but I figured I wouldn't know many of the clients I saw over the next two weeks since I was on a different schedule now than I normally was. I'd see my regulars again, and then, for now, I'd enjoy having new people to share my time with.

He was young, and, being Denobelas, like Monroe, he was quite beautiful too, with striking blond hair that reminded me of sunshine, and freckles running over his cheeks and shoulders, as wild as the blue eyes he watched me with. He was nervous, at first, though I was used to that from people who were new to coming to us. He made the time go quickly as I soothed his worries and kissed him until he couldn't breathe. By the end of our session, we were both smiling, and he was laid out over me like a warm, smothering blanket.

He hadn't told me his name, though I had asked for it as something to call him. He'd barely spoken to me at all, which I figured was simply part of being nervous. We kissed at my door before we said good-bye. I opened it to let him out and frowned at the man standing against the other side of the hallway, quietly watching me and glowering as if he had any right to judge me for what I did with my life or my time.

The Denobelas boy left me, still smiling, and I rolled my eyes at Emmanuel before shutting the door in his face. I expected to have a session with him after I'd had a chance to shower and clean up the room, but that was apparently not to be the case as a gruff man who was deliciously rough with me knocked on my door an hour later.

CHAPTER
FIVE

I DIDN'T see Emmanuel for another week, and by then I had met so many new people and heard so many stories, that I'd pushed him to the back of my mind. This group of men was a different sort than the ones I'd grown so used to in Asiq. They were younger, laughed louder, and played with each other far more openly than the men I knew in my rotation.

I fit in easily, dancing on stage between two of them, the music washing over my skin just as their hands did, quietly seeking out my sensitive places. But I was Sythe, so all of me was sensitive, and because of that, I had quickly found myself to be a favorite partner among them. I kissed the one in front of me while the other dragged his fingers down my spine, making my skin pulse with heat and my nerves flare brightly.

It was then, while my lips were sealed against another man's, that I saw Emmanuel quietly staring at me. He may have thought there had been something more between us when he came to see me on the station, but now I saw that he clearly knew better by the dark look in his eyes. Someone came to brush against him, trying to get his attention and his time, but Emmanuel didn't look away from me.

He wasn't the only client we were showing off for, not by a long shot, as they crowded into the dark room, their attentions all focused on the stage in the middle where I danced with the two men. But he was the only one I noticed.

The song ended, and another immediately started up again. I excused myself from the stage, despite the protests of both the dancers and the customers around me, and headed straight toward him. I grabbed us each a drink from a stand next to the bar on my way, something light blue and potent by the smell of it, and handed it to him as soon as I was close enough to.

"Hello, Emmanuel," I said brightly. I was flushed from dancing and glad to let him look his fill as I caught his gaze roaming over my exposed upper body.

He gave me a nod and sipped his drink. "You looked to be having fun."

"I generally do."

"Last week as well." He took another sip, and I had my first taste of the drink in my hand. It wasn't my favorite, as I preferred a fruit mix in mine, but it wasn't bad either. And it would get the clients loosened up and willing to spend their credits on us.

I shrugged blandly. "I usually have fun with all of my clients. I'm not paid to be miserable with them. Did you come here to see someone?"

"You," he said, startling me with his boldness and making me smile. Maybe the potent drink was working on him as well as on every other patron in Asiq.

I put the drink aside, though I'd barely touched it, and laced my fingers through his. "Then come on back with me."

I'd barely closed the door behind us when he grabbed me and pinned me to the wall, sealing his mouth against mine. I smiled against his lips as I felt powerful knowing that I'd gotten that strong of a reaction out of him just by dancing with two strangers. I wondered what kind of a response he'd give me if he saw me with someone else, the way some of my clients liked to do. It was a kink, but not that unusual of one, and like all the other kinks I serviced, I didn't mind that one at all.

He brought his mouth to the side of my neck, sucking on me as hard as he could, more than hard enough to bruise someone with lighter skin, though it would barely show up against my purple skin, and I dug my fingers into his arms. He pushed himself between my thighs, and I felt him hard and ready for me, even before he began to rub against me as if he was desperate to have me.

It was a nice change from how he'd been before, but it didn't feel real for some reason. The standoffish bounty hunter who couldn't stand to be touched by me had somehow become desperate to have me in the span of a few weeks? That didn't seem right at all.

I gave him a light shove, then a harder one when he didn't respond to the first. That got him off me but only enough that he fell back on the bed and grinned at me as if I was playing with him. I could play. I spent most of my days doing just that. I jumped on him, straddling his hips. He'd been in control when he had me against the wall, but now I had him pinned, and I was almost concerned for him.

"What brought this change?" I asked as he put his hands on my stomach, then down to my hips, holding me in place above him where he could rub against me.

He didn't answer me, just kept moving my hips over his, seeking his own pleasure. For my part, I kept my hands at my sides. I wanted him, I'd probably always want him, but I needed to know what was going on first. Some people would have simply taken his change at face value. Since he was keeping me alive, I wanted to make sure I didn't piss him off if something was actually going on with him that I needed to know about. If there wasn't then we'd be naked together, and I'd welcome what happened after that point.

"Emmanuel," I said, covering his hands with mine. "What's going on?"

"Want you…. Need you…." He grunted as he pressed against me, seemingly desperate for friction and his own release.

Shaking my head, I moved my hands off his and pressed the little button on the underside of my com, the one that would send an emergency pulse directly to Monroe's com on his wrist. I knew, from seeing it with someone else, that my location would then pop up on his com screen. I silently counted to ten, trying not to pay attention to Emmanuel as he moved under me, then turned my head as the door opened and Monroe rushed in, looking angry at first, then confused.

"There's something wrong with him," I said blandly as I tried to get off Emmanuel's lap now that I no longer had to hold him down, but he held on tightly to me, keeping us connected.

"Nothing's wrong with me," he snapped, his voice sounding rough as he groaned.

I rolled my eyes and grabbed the thumbs on each of his hands, twisting his hands by having control over his thumbs and getting him to let go of me. "Monroe is going to look you over."

I got off his lap and sat down next to him on the bed instead as Monroe came forward and pressed a tester against the side of Emmanuel's neck. Just like with us, the small silver instrument read everything there was to know about Emmanuel's body, including whatever it was that was making him act crazy.

Monroe looked at the tester and shook his head. "Aside from wanting sex, which isn't anything that I'd consider to be wrong with a person, there's nothing that the tester can find going on with him."

I looked down at Emmanuel to find him watching me too. "So this is just you wanting me?" I asked him. I was more than a little surprised.

He nodded and sat up. "Yes. But now that you've brought in another person, and, in the process, humiliated me, I don't think I'm interested anymore." Emmanuel started to get off the bed, but I put my hand on his chest, pushing him back down.

"We're fine here, Monroe," I told my boss even though I was looking at Emmanuel.

"If you're sure...." Of course he would hesitate. I'd called for an emergency, and there wasn't any. It wasn't something I did often, and he was likely skeptical. Maybe he even thought Emmanuel was somehow manipulating me into saying everything was okay when it wasn't. That wasn't the case here, though. I'd simply misread the situation.

"I am."

I must have been able to convince him somehow, because Monroe left a second later, leaving me alone with Emmanuel again. "I'm sorry," I said as I slid myself back on his lap.

He nodded and brought his hands to my hips again. He moved against me, just as before, but with not nearly the same level of need as he'd shown me only a few minutes ago. "I want you."

I could tell that. I rested my hands on his lower stomach, letting him rub me against him and find his own pace and pleasure, in whatever way he was comfortable with.

"I want to be inside you, even if you are a whore."

My scowl was immediate. "I'm not a whore. I'm an aspasian. Say it with me, Emmanuel. A-space-ian." He didn't, of course, instead choosing to roll with me so that I was under him on the bed and he could slide against me.

"I saw you dancing with those two tonight, and I heard you with that boy last week. You act like a whore with them," he growled against my neck.

My need for him was gone, but fortunately, I didn't have to want the people I was with in order to help them have a good time with me. And our meetings were part of our deal, though sex wasn't. But I wouldn't turn him away. I needed him not to kill me too much for that.

I turned my head to the side and rested my hands on his shoulders. I let myself open up for him, but only a little. He'd pissed me off with his name-calling too much for me to give him any more than that. But even that little bit was enough to have me gasping as heat rose in my cheeks and along my neck, straight down my stomach to my crotch, where he was still pressed heavily against me.

"I hate that I want you, a whore," he ground out against my neck before biting down on me.

He could hate wanting me all he said; I hated that my hands tightened on his shoulders on their own as that bit of pain laced through the side of my neck, and I tightened my thighs against his hips. He was perfectly hard against me, letting me know it wasn't just in my imagination, but that was hardly a consolation prize when he'd called me a whore more than once in our short session together.

I didn't need much from the people I saw while I was in Asiq, but a bit of respect would have been nice to get from him. I didn't think that was too much to ask for.

He moved back from me and took himself out a minute or two later. I didn't get up, and I certainly didn't help him as I would have with any of my other clients. Emmanuel wasn't a client; he was simply someone I was paying not to kill me, and to keep other people from killing me. He came on the sheets with a low moan, but he didn't look in my direction as he did so. Instead he simply wiped his hand off on the sheet too, and put himself away. He was cleaned up a few minutes later, and I started stripping the bed before he'd even left the room. It was rude of me, but then again, he'd called me a whore more than once, and I was sick of it.

For his part, he looked ashamed of himself as he stood there watching me toss the sheets into the steamer compartment then grab new ones out of the hidden drawer along the wall. "I should not have done that," he said once I'd finished getting the bed ready for my next client. I still needed to shower and scrub myself before I could see anyone again, but at least the room was cleaned up.

"Done what? Called me a whore?" I snapped at him.

He looked unfazed by my anger. "I should not have enjoyed myself with you."

I bit back the harsh words I wanted to say to him and instead shrugged. "Well, if you're all done, the door is right there. I'm going to shower. I have more clients tonight. Don't be here when I get out."

I'd also never showered between clients when the client was still in the room, but Emmanuel deserved my rudeness as far as I was concerned. I started the water—a real shower was what Monroe preferred we use—not the steam I had on the station, and heard the door close, presumably behind Emmanuel.

CHAPTER
SIX

THE NEXT time I saw Emmanuel was nearly a month later, while I was on Asiq for my last few days before going home to the station. I'd survived six weeks of being an aspasian without needing a break from it. Monroe looked surprised, and I was a bit too. But I wasn't tired or bored in any way.

When he came in through the front door, I was unwrapping a piece of chocolate I'd snatched from one of the bowls Monroe kept in every room. They were supposed to be mostly for the clients, but we could eat them too. Monroe seemed to have a never-ending supply of them around Asiq, and I enjoyed them whenever I had a moment to. Beside me was a glass of tropical fruits mixed together with cream to create a lovely smoothie. Like the chocolates and the water-based shower, it was another indulgence I didn't get to enjoy on the station.

I'd already asked to stay on Asiq for another four weeks, but Monroe had told me to go home and sleep awhile. My account was quite a bit fuller after the two extra weeks in Asiq, and I felt no worse for the extra wear on my body. In fact, I felt good enough to smile at Emmanuel and lift my glass to him in a silent salute when he passed through the weapons detectors and was let into the front lobby of Asiq.

He still had to get through the front desk to be able to reach me, unless he was using the back door like I'd suspected he had the first night we'd met. I was surprised the detectors hadn't found the neutralizers I saw hanging from each of his hips, but perhaps Monroe had programed the scanners to ignore them whenever Emmanuel came through. That was the most likely scenario, I realized, just as the young man at the front counter waved Emmanuel into the lounge. Technically, since I was out in the open, I was on duty and open for business.

Emmanuel sat down heavily next to me, and I glanced over at him as I sipped my drink. "Hello. Can I get you anything?" Like an appointment with someone else he could call a whore besides myself. I had to be nice to him since I was at Asiq. But I didn't have to fall all over him and pretend he was the greatest thing in the universe, which he certainly wasn't. Not to me at least. Maybe someone out there loved him. Certainly he had parents, or he'd had them at one time. Maybe even a wife or a husband in the universe somewhere. I didn't know, and I didn't much care either.

"One of what you're drinking?" he asked.

I nodded and got to my feet to make him one. In the early afternoon, when we weren't at all busy at Asiq, I was both bartender and entertainer. There were a few other guys sitting around the lounge, hoping for clients to come strolling in, but Asiq really didn't get started until hours later as the first of the suns started to go down. The artificial sun was always on, providing light but not much heat. It was a nice break from the tropical temperatures of Wish.

Finished with his drink, I brought it back to him and set it down on a low table next to him. I'd been sitting a few seats away from him, and once I went back to my seat, I was glad for the distance. That was until he patted the seat next to him, inviting me to sit closer. I couldn't be rude to him in front of the other guys who worked in Asiq, though if we'd been alone, I wouldn't have gotten up at all.

As much as I didn't like him, part of me wanted to mess with him a bit. He didn't like wanting me, well I could work with that. I perched on the arm of the comfortable chair he sat in, crossing my legs and easily balancing myself as I brushed my foot against his calf. After years of doing this, I knew it looked innocent. I was well aware of how to flirt and tease, and as I caught Emmanuel watching me, I could tell he wasn't unaffected.

I sipped my drink and found him openly staring at my mouth, at my exposed chest. It warmed me, though I realized I was playing a dangerous game with a man who could still turn on me in an instant.

"Are all of your markings different?"

His question surprised me. "All Sythe?" I asked. He nodded, confirming what I'd thought he'd been asking me. "Yes. You've never seen one of us naked before?" We all had purple skin and inky black hair, but the yellow markings were individual to each of us. I only had a few slender slashes on my cheeks and shoulders. My brother had many more, his golden markings going down his chest to his finish along his ribs.

He flushed a little, the pink tint barely noticeable under the silver of his skin. "I haven't seen any of you with your shirts off before I met you. Tied there to the bed as you were. Looking helpless, though I know now that you hardly were."

I smiled. "No, I wasn't helpless. I'd have been stupid to put myself in a position that I couldn't get out of, regardless of how long I've known the client. What's your fantasy?" He was dangerous to play with, and I saw by the flash of anger in his eyes that asking him that question was a problem for him as well. I didn't play fair, though, and in Asiq, I wasn't afraid of much.

"I don't have one."

That had to be a lie. Everyone had at least one fantasy, and part of the fun of my job was getting to explore those with the people I was with. Risking certain death, I slid myself onto his lap so that I was facing him. I didn't touch him except for with my thighs, though, as I sipped my smoothie through the wide straw. "Everyone does."

He shook his head, denying my words, but I did notice him resting his hand gently on the top of my hip. He could deny wanting me all he felt like, but if he really didn't want me around, he would have pushed me off his lap, not made contact with me like he was. I gave him a quick smile and continued to drink the overly sweet concoction. It was a good distraction so that I didn't end up putting my hands on him too.

"Everyone you know may, but I don't. My fantasies involve taking out targets and making sure I stay alive long enough to enjoy the bounties." He tightened his hand on my hip, and I leaned toward him a little. If he didn't know I was interested, he had to have been really dense. I may not have liked who he was or how absolutely rude he could be at times, but that didn't mean I would refuse having him in my bed. Liking someone and wanting to have sex with them weren't always the same thing, especially not in my line of work.

Putting my now empty drink aside on a nearby table, I leaned over him, giving him my neck and remembering his teeth on my skin. I shivered and wanted that again. The rest of it had been a mess, but I could fix that. I was quick to forgive and easily gave second chances to people I wanted to experience more of. "Surely there's something you want.... Something I can help you with." I'd dropped my voice as low as I could, making myself soft and, I hoped, easy for him to want.

"I want...," he whispered as he looked up at me.

"Yes?"

He licked his lips, and I arched forward, taking his face between my hands. He had small nubs along his cheeks, not nearly the hard spikes of his shoulders and arms that were almost like body armor, these were merely bumps under his skin, and I took my time running my thumbs over them while I held his face.

Someone cleared their throat behind me, and I looked over my shoulder to find Monroe standing there, watching us. "You've been booked for an appointment."

I nodded and slid off Emmanuel's lap. If he'd been a regular client, Monroe would have never interrupted us, but then again, if he'd been a client at all, I would have had him down for an appointment, and I wouldn't have been sitting on his lap, taking my time seducing him as I had been.

"Thanks for letting me know," I told Monroe. I started toward the hallways that led to our rooms, so that I could get ready for the client, but Emmanuel grabbed my wrist, stopping me. "Yes?"

"I want to watch you with him."

His softly spoken request had me blushing as I smiled down at him. "I don't have sex with every person I have sessions with." Emmanuel looked uncertain of himself as he let go of my wrist.

"Why would you want to anyway? You were fairly upset the last time you saw me even kiss someone," I reminded him.

He nodded and sat back, leaning away from me. "I was. Maybe seeing you whoring yourself out will make me stop wanting you all the time."

And there it was. Again. I shook my head and silently walked away from him. I didn't have time to help him work out his issues. Monroe said something quietly to Emmanuel, then he was behind me.

"What did you say to him?" I asked Monroe.

He came up beside me. "That the next time he spoke to you or anyone else in my establishment that way, I would throw him out."

That made me happy. Good ol' Monroe, sticking up for us, as always. "See you in a bit."

I tried not to think about Emmanuel as I showered and readied myself for my next client. I knew this one and what he would want, and if Emmanuel wanted to see me whoring myself to someone, as he put it, Mr. Diab would be a good example. He was unfalteringly rough to the point of nearly being malicious, and he was one of the few people that Monroe allowed to skirt that line.

He wasn't given that leeway because of his money. Instead, it was because of my confidence in him. I'd vouched for Mr. Diab more than once, and though he often left me bruised, he was never cruel to me. I was, however, the only person in Monroe's employ that Mr. Diab was allowed to spend time with. I chose to think that Monroe believed I was strong enough to handle a customer like him.

This time with Mr. Diab was no different as I lay under him with my hands curled into the sheets and riding the thin line of pain as it sometimes, though far too rarely for my sake, crossed into the side of pleasure. He must have wanted more from me, because he grabbed my hands and clamped them against the small of my back, his leathery hands gripping me tightly until he was done with me.

Only then was he gentle as he released me and ran his hands down my back as if trying to soothe away the pain he'd brought me. I was breathing heavily, as was he, and for a few quiet moments, we simply sat there together, watching each other. He didn't kiss me, but he did take my hand and rub his thumb over my knuckles. Without a word he began getting dressed again, and I rolled out my shoulders, groaning a little as I heard the left one pop.

"I wish I could take you away from all this," he said as he finished putting his pants back on.

I'd heard that line before, dozens of times, and it still surprised me that people thought that way about me, as if I was miserable every second that I was in Asiq. The reality was that I was happiest when I was there, not whatever their delusions about me were. "I'm not a prisoner here, Mr. Diab. I enjoy what I do."

"Even with me?"

His quiet, uncertain question had me smirking. "Yes, especially with you." I got up, mindful of my own nudity but not caring about it in the least, and kissed his cheek. "Take care, Mr. Diab. I hope to see you again soon."

He smacked my butt before I could finish getting my robe on, and I laughed, the sound completely genuine. I was great at acting, at faking around people I didn't particularly like, but Mr. Diab wasn't one of those people that I had to force myself to be around. He caused me pain, but he seemed sorry for it as soon as we were done, as if he couldn't believe what he'd been capable of.

That was another thing I had become used to in my line of work. People came to us because they had needs that their partners could not fulfill. I'd been asked to belittle some men, to play nursemaid to others, and to let some, like Mr. Diab, get rough with me. I had limits, but from what I could tell, they were far more flexible than most people out there in the world.

Everyone needed release, in one way or another, and I was happy to supply that for my customers. In this small way, I felt as if I was helping them in their normal, everyday lives.

"Take care of yourself, Corbin. I plan to visit you again in a month."

I smiled at him and went to get the door for him now that he'd finished getting dressed. "I look forward to our next session. Fly safe."

He touched my cheek as he left the room. I never experienced release with him, but I chose to think that giving someone else pleasure, even when I found none for myself, was fine in its own way. I certainly didn't begrudge Mr. Diab, or any of my other clients, for focusing on their own needs and not mine. We weren't lovers, after all.

CHAPTER SEVEN

EMMANUEL SURPRISED me by knocking on my door as soon as I'd stepped out of the shower. Expecting it to be Monroe, I put on my robe and only briefly glanced through the peephole. But there Emmanuel stood, right outside my door, looking annoyed.

I tried not to sigh as I opened the door just wide enough to talk to him. I hadn't cleaned the room or changed the sheets yet, and I was sure I had more clients waiting, so I absolutely did not have time for whatever Emmanuel thought he was going to get out of me.

"Yes?" I practically snapped at him.

"May I come in?"

"No."

"Corbin…." He sounded nearly as frustrated as I felt.

I shook my head. "You're not coming in here. The room isn't clean."

"Fine." He gave me a little smile, though it looked far more wicked than friendly. "Why is it that you aren't afraid of me?"

I laughed and realized a second or two later that I shouldn't have been so loud, not unless I wanted to draw attention to us. Which I certainly did not want to do.

"I am. Believe me, Emmanuel, I know my own mortality, and you've proven how easily you can get into my home, and my life. I'm not stupid. I know you can kill me."

"You are a strange man." He shook his head, as if he was having trouble figuring me out. I felt the same way about him.

"What do you want?" I tried not to sound as exhausted with him as I felt. There were only so many times I could go around in circles with him before I'd lost all sense of reason.

"I'm your next client."

I pursed my lips and willed the instant rise in my anger to come down. He was an idiot, but he wasn't really being cruel to me. Monroe may have wanted to throw him out for his continued use of the word "whore" when he was around us, but, although the word annoyed me, I would much rather be alive and hearing it, than dead because he thought I'd ended our bargain.

"You're going to have to wait a minute. I'm not ready to see another client so soon." I'd already told him the room wasn't clean, and he'd simply have to accept that. Clients weren't allowed in messy rooms. Each of them deserved a fresh place to be in, to give more credibility to the fantasy that they were the only one I saw, that they were it for me. It was a lie, but it was one clients seemed to enjoy as I pretended I cared deeply for each of them.

He nodded, stepping away from the door, and I closed it quietly in his face. I was ready ten minutes later and opened the door to find him standing there, waiting for me with his hands behind his back and his legs spread. He looked alert but still relaxed in a way, and though he didn't move his mouth at all, I would swear he was smiling inside from the way the skin around his eyes crinkled when our gazes met.

"Are you coming in, then? Or did you want to talk in the hallway?" Monroe would have never allowed that, but I wanted to see what Emmanuel would say to me.

"I didn't say I wanted to talk to you." He walked past me as I felt my cheeks heat, and I was glad that my skin was so much darker than my brother's was. Where he had yellow on his cheeks, which did show his blush, my purple skin only became a little darker when I was embarrassed, or in this case, completely turned on as I smiled at his back.

I closed the door behind him and leaned against it. "If you don't want to talk, then what do you want with me today?" I asked him. I had my answer a second later when he turned around to face me and began undoing the tiny buttons of his armored vest.

Normally I would have rushed up and helped a client undress himself unless I'd been told not to. He hadn't said anything of the sort, but I wanted to watch him strip off his clothes. He was precise, as if he was afraid of damaging a single thread, and his movements held none of the rush I was used to.

He went down to his pants, baring his upper body for my curious view, and my smile instantly died on my lips at the sight of the scars that covered his silvery skin. He hadn't turned around for me yet, which was good since I needed a minute to get myself under control. I'd seen plenty of scars before. I'd been an aspasian for the last twenty years, and in that time had been around hundreds of people. Scars were nothing new to me. But in the quantity he had them, where they almost appeared to make a pattern over his skin, making his silvery skin nearly pink in some places, I had no idea what to do, or say.

He turned around and must have seen something in my expression, because he quickly came forward and kissed me. It was a gentle kiss, one I used to distract myself. I pitied him for the pain he must have gone through to get those morbid decorations to his skin, but I didn't want him to know I pitied him as much as I did.

Emmanuel helped me take off my shirt before bringing his hands to my cheeks, cupping my face. And yet our kiss remained gentle, chaste even. It wasn't something I was used to, or could have expected from him or anyone else. I reached for the front of his pants, but he jerked his hips away from me.

"No. I don't want that," he said, releasing me as I simply stared up at him.

"Then what?"

He gave me a sad little smile. "Do you give massages?"

I wanted to smirk at him, because, really, I did everything. I'd stand on my head for twenty minutes if that was what a client wanted from me. And I had. But with him looking at me as if he expected me to refuse him on even that simple, nonsexual act, I could do little more

48

than give him a nod. "Of course. Waist up?" I guessed, since he'd refused to let me take off his pants.

"Please."

That wasn't a problem for me at all. I took his hand and brought him over to the bed with its fresh sheets and perfectly folded corners. Not many clients noticed the care we took with the rooms, but Monroe had his standards, and after so many years here, nearly half my life actually, being neat up to his standards had become like second nature to me.

He laid down on his stomach, pulling one of the many fluffy pillows under his chin and wrapping his arms around it. I grabbed a bit of the citrus-scented lotion we had in each of the rooms and rubbed it between my palms, getting it warm for him. Once he'd seemed to settle into the bed, I spread my thighs over his hips, settling onto the firm cushion of his butt.

"Anywhere that hurts right now?" I asked him. I'd given plenty of massages in my life but never to a Nafsu, or to someone as beat up as he was. If I were as scarred as he was, a massage would have probably hurt me. There is no way it wouldn't have since my nerves were far more sensitive than other people's were. We Sythe were special like that.

"No. Wherever you want to touch, go ahead."

I nodded and started at the base of his spine. He jumped under my hands, though, as if he wasn't expecting me to touch him. "Is the lotion cold?"

"I haven't had a massage before," he explained, making me frown. They were a normal part of my life here in Asiq. But maybe that was because Monroe spoiled us beyond the water we got to drink and the real showers we were able to take.

"I'll go slow," I promised him as I began lightly running my hands over his back and up to his shoulders. I didn't use my normal pressure, instead simply touching him for now. The bumps along his shoulders were hard against my hands, but they weren't sharp like I'd expected them to be. I smiled as I thought of how silly it would be if they were. He'd never be able to wear any clothes since they would be cut up all the time. "May I ask about your scars?"

"If you want to."

I did want to. But I didn't want to make him uncomfortable, and he sounded like he was starting to fall asleep under me. "Never mind. I'll ask another time," I decided.

"I got them all from various bounties. Sometimes people like to fight back. Like you did," he filled in for me.

I pressed a little harder, running my thumbs down his spine and leaning over his back. He was built, not that I wasn't since I did like to keep in shape, but his shoulders must have been a good three inches wider than mine on either side. He was an impressive sight, and one I enjoyed staring at, especially when he couldn't stop me from indulging myself.

He arched under my hands, and I pressed a bit deeper at the base of his spine, figuring I must have hit a tight spot. I got a soft groan out of him in return, which made me smile. "Have you ever refused a bounty?"

"Yes. I don't hunt down innocent people."

His answer was so simple, and yet, I was innocent. At least in my mind I was. "You came after me," I reminded him.

"You have sex with people for credits."

Rolling my eyes, I continued to work on the tight spot at the base of his spine. "Yes, I do. Sometimes ridiculous amounts of credits that, before I became an aspasian, I hadn't made even after a month of working in the mines. You can think what you want, but I enjoy my work, and right now, you seem to be enjoying it too. Or did you forget that this is part of what I do too?"

"I didn't forget. This is a gray area that I'm willing to overlook."

"Small miracles," I said, a bit snidely. I was amused on some level that the thing that benefited him was allowed to be overlooked. But I understood it too. I did have sex with people, lots of people, for money. It was an unconventional life, but it was one that I loved, and I would defend it against him or anyone else.

"You know that I don't have sex with everyone that I bring into this room, right? I told you that before, but maybe it'll start sinking in after today."

"What percent?" he asked me, as if I was supposed to keep track of that.

It took me a few seconds to make even half a guess. "Maybe 70 percent? That I do have sex with." Wish was a pleasure planet. What people found pleasure in was as varied as anything else about them. I didn't judge; I simply accepted, and if I couldn't give them what they needed, then I got in touch with Monroe with a quick comcall. If someone in Asiq couldn't fulfill their needs, he'd always been good about referring them to another brothel that could. Customers were just that important to him, and many of the ones he referred out eventually came back to us for other services, even if their new brothel could give them that.

He gave me a little sigh. "That number seems like a lot. That's what? A hundred people? Since you started working here?"

The number was at least triple that, but I'd stopped counting a long time ago. "I didn't lie before. You're going to have to go higher than that."

He shivered, and I imagined that he was disgusted with me. "How are those numbers compared to your kills?"

"About the same probably. And I've been doing this as long as you've been an aspasian."

I leaned down and kissed him between his thick shoulders, figuring he deserved a little bit of kindness from me. "Thank you for not calling me a whore."

"I considered it. But I'm enjoying this too much for you to call Monroe and have him throw me out."

That made me laugh. The com on his wrist beeped, and he put an earpiece in his ear. I didn't care that I wasn't able to listen in on the other half of his conversation. I more thought it was rude that he would be answering a comcall during his massage at all.

"Hello…. No, I haven't had any luck finding him yet. I thought I did, but it turned out to be a different Sythe. They're fairly common in this sector."

51

I froze on top of him, being smart enough to figure out that he was likely talking about me. Emmanuel got up on his elbows and shifted his weight a bit. I thought he might have wanted to sit up, so I moved off his butt to kneel next to him on the bed as he continued his conversation.

"Affirmative. I'll continue to look for him. Yes, the normal delivery method of proof will be fine for me too. Thank you, sir." He ended the call and took the earpiece out before sitting up. He turned toward me, and I expected him to go back on our deal, to try to grab me again, but he only gave me another of his sad little smiles.

"The massage was nice. Thank you. I need to be going now."

I frowned at him, wanting a lot more information out of him than just that. "Was the call about me?"

"Yes. You're the only Sythe I've been assigned to hunt down so far. Which, honestly, is a bit surprising. You'd think, given how you are rumored to be in bed, that I would have been given the command from a jealous husband or jilted lover long before Senator Saunders decided to give that order."

He'd told me before, but I had to ask this question again. "And if you don't give him proof of my death soon, then what? He'll send someone else to kill me off? Right?"

Emmanuel nodded and got off the bed to begin putting on his shirt and vest again. "Yes. And, before you get any ideas you think are smart, he won't just ask for a picture of you lying there in blood that can be easily faked. I send my employers a vid of the body, but then I also bring them a part of whoever I was supposed to kill. A distinctive tattoo, usually. Less often the head."

I shuddered and sat back on my heels, suddenly not feeling so great. "You must have a very strong stomach."

Now dressed, Emmanuel simply shrugged at me. "I've become immune to it. Just like their screams and begging. There is very little that holds my interest anymore outside of earning credits and spending them."

He sounded cold and callous about it, and I thought he was. But I also realized many people would have likely developed that kind of tolerance for the acts he committed after so many years of doing them.

"What if the senator never stops looking for me?" I quietly asked him.

"Then I will keep protecting you, and not killing you at the same time, until your money runs out."

He didn't smile at me to let me know he was joking in any way, and for that I was both sickened, and, in a way, relieved. I could take him at face value, and despite kissing me and the other intimate moments we'd shared, the second I was no longer able to give him the credits I'd promised him, he would collect the bounty on me.

I nodded, understanding him completely. When he came over to kiss my lips, I gave him my cheek instead. He gave me a gentle kiss close to the line of my jaw and gave my long ponytail a gentle tug. "I won't let anything happen to you," he promised me.

"As long as I can pay you for the foreseeable future," I reminded him coldly.

He released my hair and ran his fingertips up my shoulder and down my arm, leaving off at my elbow. "I would take no pleasure in your death. I want you to know that."

I looked up at him, meeting his blue eyes, and wishing I was strong enough to hit him and actually make him hurt a little. But I didn't hit clients, at least not when they weren't trying to kill me. If he turned his guns on me again, I would absolutely give him everything I had. "I would rather that you not kill me at all."

He brought his hand to my left cheek, cupping my face, and I let myself open up a little. I'd been on edge around him, reserving myself while I was with him, and so I'd been clamped down as tightly as I could be. It felt good to relax for a second, to let my nerves reach out for that connection as warmth began to move through me. Being open was our natural state as we connected with those around us. I couldn't stop the sigh that fell from my mouth as he brushed his lips across my forehead in the gentlest of kisses.

"If I don't, someone else will. And they will not have my morals."

His threat was clear, and I knew he wasn't lying. "If Saunders was killed, would the bounty on my head go away? And the ones on everyone else's as well?" I asked.

He released my face, and I felt my nerves reaching back out for him, as if my skin was begging him silently to come back, to stay and touch me a little while longer. I wanted to him to do just that, but I would not beg him for it.

"You don't have the kind of credits that would be needed for that," he said as he took a step toward the door, apparently ready to leave me.

I likely didn't, but his answer wasn't a "no."

"Give me a price," I demanded.

Emmanuel thought for a moment, then nodded as if coming to some kind of conclusion, like he had a running total of how much each person he knew would be worth to kill. As far as I knew, that's exactly what he had going on in his head. It wouldn't have surprised me. "Twenty-five thousand credits, in one lump sum, and I would bring you back his head."

Though that was quite a bit of money, it was less than Thierry's education had been when he'd gone off to be a pilot years before. They'd since raised their tuition, again, and I was thankful I had no more siblings to worry about now that he was grown and making a name for himself in systems far from this one.

"I'll think on it," I told him, already wondering if Monroe would reconsider his stance on not giving us loans. He'd refused me once before, but that had been for a part that needed repaired on my shuttle. This situation was substantially different, as my life was involved now. "How about you kill him simply because you like me alive?"

Emmanuel gave me a smile. "I don't like you more than the credits he offered me to kill you." He winked, but that didn't mean a whole lot when I knew he was telling me the truth.

I rolled my eyes and got off the bed so that I could show him out. "I hope you buy something really great with the credits you get from giving him my head," I said sarcastically as I opened the door for him, silently telling him he could go.

He smirked at me, gave me another kiss on my cheek, and left my room. I wanted to slam the door behind him since I was absolutely angry with him, but I didn't need Monroe storming in to see what was wrong with me or to have my boss be angry with me.

CHAPTER EIGHT

BACK HOME and completely relaxed in my apartment, I was happy to be binging on a handful of chocolates I'd taken from Asiq. I had some music from the Mian system playing through my com, and it was very good to simply lay on my couch, hang my feet over the side, and eat as many of the sweets as I wanted to.

Thierry had loved these little bites of goodness when he'd been in Asiq and, for once, I was kind of glad he wasn't around so that I didn't have to share with him. After our parents had died in the accident, when I'd been much younger and Thierry was still a child, I'd shared everything with him. I never thought I'd be sharing the place I worked with him, though, which still bothered me sometimes. He'd auctioned off his virginity to Monroe, and somehow they'd fallen in love after that. The guy I'd given my virginity to, if I knew where he was anymore, I might have hired Emmanuel to go take care of for me. Probably not, but when he'd first broken my heart some twenty-plus years ago, I would have heavily considered it.

I liked to think I was more mature and had a better set of morals now, despite what Emmanuel thought of me. Thinking about him made my mood sour even more than chocolates could help unfortunately. I didn't like that he made me curious about him, or that I found myself attracted to him. The only thing that I found redeemable in him at all was how easy he was to understand. As long as he considered me guilty of something, he'd kill me if the price was right. It was a horrible way to be thought of, and it bothered me greatly, but part of me understood his way of thinking because I had my own set of morals too.

As an aspasian, I was able to choose who I was with, and I could refuse people who didn't fit into what I wanted. Monroe didn't like it when we did that, and I saw no reason to since he only let select clientele into Asiq to begin with, but I had that option. Emmanuel chose to kill guilty people, I chose to spend time with people who were nice to me and generally respected me. There were men in Asiq who enjoyed having sex with women. That was one choice Monroe was fine with us making. Age, size, race... we were expected to overlook those things in our clients, and I couldn't remember a time, even from when I'd first come to Asiq, that those traits had mattered at all to me.

I liked people who smiled at me, who spoke to me with kindness, and who sat down with me and discussed what they wanted from me. I had plenty of regulars because of the time I spent with them during our first meetings. My job was all about bringing their fantasies to life, and I absolutely enjoyed doing that, even if some of them had no idea what their fantasies actually were.

Maybe it was that difference that annoyed me about Emmanuel's view of my life and what I did. Yes, I did have sex with people, a lot of people actually, for money. But it wasn't just the sex that I enjoyed. I'd been taught how to sing from someone who wanted to start giving lessons but needed a student to practice on. Dancing was second nature to me from all the clients who had simply wanted a partner to hold them.

And here Emmanuel was, assuming I simply stripped down and laid back whenever someone came into my room at Asiq. I rolled my eyes and popped another chocolate into my mouth. I decided to call Thierry instead of spending any more time thinking about Emmanuel. My brother, I was sure, would be a much better place for my thoughts to go than the bounty hunter who, if not for the drop in credits in my account since that morning, might be coming for me right then.

I put the earpiece in my ear out of habit even though I was alone, and called my brother up on the com.

"Hey," he said instantly. The connection was dim, a sure sign he was still far away. I missed him so much when we were talking like this.

"Hi. I'm having chocolate. Thought you should know."

He groaned at my teasing him, and I smiled. "Monroe's? Tell me you aren't bragging about having Monroe's chocolates. I couldn't take that."

Laughing, I unwrapped another, slowly so that he could hear it, then bit down hard on the solid piece before swallowing it. "I am. How've you been?"

"Clearly not as good as you with your chocolates and my Monroe." His voice got wispy there at the end as if he missed his lover. They hadn't seen each other for years, and I didn't know how they kept up the affection they clearly had for each other through the distance and time apart. "How is he?"

"Fine. I've been good too, in case you were wondering."

He laughed, knowing my sarcasm well enough to be able to tell that I was joking with him. "Me too. Wish I was there, though. On Wish. Ha-ha. Okay, maybe I do need to get off this ship if I'm laughing at my own bad jokes."

His voice was getting softer, harder to hear as if the ship was moving away from the nearest planet with a good com satellite. He must have been in a deep system, then. "Tell me what you're looking at," I said.

"Looking at? My shirt, actually. There's a spot on it, and I'm trying to remember if it was from breakfast or lunch. Or did you mean outside the ship?"

"Yes, outside. No one cares about your shirt." I rolled my eyes.

He chuckled. "The captain might. He likes us all to look presentable. But anyway, outside the ship I'm looking at the three moons of the planet Sentry. We took samples from the largest one yesterday and will be going to the smaller two in a few hours."

"My little brother, the explorer." I was so proud of him. I hoped he knew that.

"My big brother, the glamorous aspasian, eating chocolates in the lap of luxury while getting to spend time with the man I love."

He sounded jealous, and I smiled. "You could come back for a while. Take some time off to stay in your home system for a month, maybe longer."

"I can't." In his voice, though, I heard how much he wanted to. "Why not?"

He hesitated, and I wondered what secrets he would try to hide from me now. When he was in school, he'd pulled that kind of a stunt, but we were well past that in my mind. "I promised Monroe I'd do a lot with my life before I came back. I'm still exploring, still finding new places, meeting new civilizations. I'll be there soon, I promise, but I can't see him until I'm done, until I'd be satisfied with only sector jobs and never again jumping between gates and seeing new worlds."

For once Monroe's relationship with my brother made absolute sense, and I wished that he'd told me some of that sooner. Maybe then I wouldn't have been so worried about him. No, actually, I would have still been worried. He was my little brother, and I would have always been worried about him. I was sure of that. I'd raised him after our parents died and had been responsible for him for years before he left for the academy at twenty. "Are you close to being done?"

"Yes. I don't think I'll be out here more than another six months. The drive to see and do things is waning, and my need to be in one place, to have a real home again, is taking over. For the past two years, this research ship, the *Barton*, has been my home, but it doesn't feel like a home. It feels like a ship, the same way the station you live on feels like a ship. On Wish there's sunlight and fresh air, fruits and bright colors."

"And Monroe," I added, knowing his mind was already there. Mine would have been too, if I loved someone.

He didn't deny it. "Yes. And Monroe."

His voice was barely audible now. "You're drifting pretty far out from the sats. Take care of yourself, Thierry. I'll hold you to coming back in less than a year. No more than that."

59

"I'll be back well before then. See you soon."

I ended the comcall and removed the earpiece. I was proud of him, and I missed him. And, knowing how much Monroe missed him too, I took out my holoscreen from my bag and opened a note to him.

Talked to Thierry. He misses you.

I wouldn't tell Monroe about Thierry promising to come back around six months from now, in case he decided to stay out a little longer. I would be disappointed but happy for him for finding something new that piqued his interest. I saw no reason to get Monroe's hopes up in case that happened, though. I remembered what it felt like to love someone, even though it had been many years for me, and I knew what it was like to be devastated when they didn't keep their promises. I didn't want that for either my brother or Monroe.

My holoscreen beeped, which was weird since I'd thought I'd put it on silent, but then I remembered that Monroe was marked as an important contact, so his messages always came to my attention. Thierry was too, but, like Monroe, I used comcalls with him more than notes.

Thank you for the update.

Monroe's message made me laugh. He was so formal, so absolutely silent about their relationship sometimes that I couldn't help wanting to make fun of him for it. We were close, but not that close, though, so I knew not to go there with him.

Of course.

I replied to him before I turned off my holoscreen and put it aside. My chocolates were nearly gone, so I settled back into the couch, relaxed, and took my time eating them. They'd have to last me until I was back in Asiq in two weeks. After so many years, I should have found a way to slow myself down instead of devouring them all within a few hours of landing on the station. But I had yet to master that skill.

I'D GONE to bed at nearly midnight, but it couldn't have been more than an hour later when I felt someone slam down on top of me. I struggled and cried out but was quickly silenced by the shot of a neutralizer gun to my chest. The last thought I could remember, before I lost consciousness, was of how much I was going to make Emmanuel pay for this as the neutralizer made every muscle in my body contract, stopping any movement and every sound I would have tried to make.

CHAPTER
NINE

I WOKE up some time later, my head feeling like it was full of Mian sweet fluff—all air and clouds and very little actual substance. Children liked it. I did not, especially when it felt like I couldn't form a thought to save my life.

My blurred vision eventually cleared, and I realized I was tied to a steel post on someone's bridge. I looked around for Emmanuel and was ready to call him out on whatever he thought he was doing. But instead of Emmanuel, the first person I saw was Mr. Diab as he turned away from the control dock and smiled at me.

"You're awake. I'm so glad." He came over to crouch beside me and undo my wrists, letting me slump forward as I rubbed my hands together to get feeling back into them. "You had me worried there for a little while. I told my men to convince you to come with them, to be gentle with you. But they did not listen to me. Don't worry. They're gone now. I don't tolerate acts like that against the people I love."

I could only stare up at him. He loved me? Since when? And when had Mr. Diab gone crazy? He'd been fond of me since we'd first met in the lounge at Asiq, but I'd never imagined…. He was staring at me, though, as if he expected some kind of an intelligent answer from me.

"Um…. Thank you." I had no idea what else to give him, but I guessed that worked because he smiled at me and leaned forward to kiss me. I wanted to give him my cheek, like I did with Emmanuel when I was annoyed with him, but Mr. Diab wasn't acting sane, and I didn't want to anger the man who had kidnapped me. Not until I had a plan to get back home at the very least. After that, I didn't much care what happened to him. In fact, I was sure that this was one person I would send Emmanuel after. And gladly too.

I let Mr. Diab kiss me and forced myself to open up to him despite the residual pain from the neutralizer blast against the center of my chest. Not lethal certainly didn't mean powerless when it came to that weapon. My nerves blazed open, and I sighed against his mouth as he slipped his tongue between my teeth.

He brought his hand to the side of my neck, and I held still, trying very hard not to jerk out of his grip as my strength slowly started to come back to me. Mercifully, he ended the kiss quickly and seemed to expect nothing more from me at that moment as he stood back up, his long coat brushing against the steel grate below us, and walked back to the control station.

His leathery skin had been rough against my face and neck, and I wished that I could rub at the spot where he'd touched me most without bringing attention to myself. "Where are we?" I asked him, trying to sound as casual as I could. Of course I didn't have my holoscreen with me, since that had been in the living room when I'd been kidnapped, which was what I was calling it despite my age, but if I had still been in possession of my holoscreen I would have contacted Emmanuel.

I could have chosen to get word to Monroe, but I didn't want to worry him or have him tell Thierry that someone had taken me from the apartment. I didn't want them involved in this either, and I knew Monroe would get himself in the middle of it. He cared about Thierry too much, and the money I brought in for him, to let something happen to me.

But this situation didn't need Monroe's touch. It needed Emmanuel's precision. I just had to play Mr. Diab long enough to get word to Emmanuel so he could come take care of this problem for me. I was cocky as I got unsteadily to my feet and made my way to a chair beside where Mr. Diab was standing.

"You'd like to know where we are?" he asked.

I nodded. I did. Because then I could tell Emmanuel where he could come get me and kill Mr. Diab. I wasn't all that much in the mood to be kidnapped, now or ever actually.

"Take a look."

I did, judging the planets I could see through the narrow window in front of me, and comparing them to everything I'd learned. "Setina system?" Mr. Diab gave me a smile, so I figured I was in the right area. Which meant that Emmanuel's chances of finding me were actually pretty good. Setina wasn't all that big of a system. One star, two inhabitable planets, each with small moon, and one planet made almost entirely of thick ice, an asteroid belt separating it from the two inhabitable planets.

Unfortunately it looked like Mr. Diab meant to hide his ship in those asteroids. Fine. I could handle that. The belt wasn't thick enough that a distress signal wouldn't get through. But they might mess with Emmanuel's readers and delay him finding me. I'd just have to play along longer.

"Mr. Diab, why are we out here?"

Clearly because he was crazy, but I wasn't about to say something like that. Not when I needed him not to kill me, or maim me, or mess me up too badly.

He put the ship on autopilot and came over to me, running his fingers through my loose hair. I loved how long it was but not how it felt when it was wild like it was right then. I didn't keep it tied back when I went to sleep, though, and I normally didn't wear clothing either since Thierry had long ago moved out, so I guess I should have been thankful that I'd fallen asleep before getting completely undressed. Otherwise this would have been much more awkward than it already was.

"Don't you know? Now we can be together. You don't have be there anymore. You can be mine. You don't have to lie or pretend. You'll be so happy here, with me. I'll make sure of it. I love you so much. And I know you love me too. You always say how good it was to see me, how you can't wait to see me again. I love hearing that from you."

He bent over and kissed me on the side of my neck, and I tried hard not to pull away as he pressed his hand to the front of my pants. He thought I didn't have to act anymore? The thing was, I was acting more now than I ever had in Asiq as I brought my hands up to his chest, letting him know I wanted him too. He'd always been on the line for me, a long-term customer who I spent time with because of the bond I'd built up with him, but one I wouldn't have been sad to see go in the least. I liked keeping my customers, most of them, and for a while that had been true of Mr. Diab. If he hadn't kidnapped me, I would have kept him in that category and, like he said, I would have been pleasant to him every single time that he came by.

But now I was trying hard not to say what was on my mind, including just how wrong he was and how disgusted I was by him and what he'd done. He moved his mouth back to mine, and I groaned against him as he continued to squeeze me. As much as I opened myself up to him, as hot as my nerves became against my skin, I couldn't force myself to react to his hand between my legs, and that seemed to bother him as he pulled back and frowned down at me.

"I'm sorry," I said, looking as pathetic and sorry as possible as I licked my lips and looked up at him. "I think the neutralizer gun might be making certain parts of me slow to come back." If he wanted me, then I'd be sure to play along and act like I wanted him too. It would make it even better when Emmanuel killed him. I reached for his pants and began to undo his buttons.

"Of course. I'm sorry that happened to you. I had them killed slowly for what they did to you. That was never part of the plan. Come, not here, my eager lover. I'll have you properly in my quarters. They're the captain's quarters, of course. I think you'll like them. Excellent views...."

His words kept going, but I was done listening to him talk as he pulled me to my feet by a strong grip on my wrist and hurried me out of the bridge. We passed a few guards, all of them heavily armed and wearing body armor, and I worried for a split-second about Emmanuel's safety when he came to rescue me. I realized, as Mr.

Diab showed me just how much he'd missed me and loved me while we were in his quarters, that there was no question in my mind that Emmanuel would come for me. He had to. He was my only hope off this ship since I had none of my things. I didn't even have my com to be able to call someone.

Fortunately, while Mr. Diab found his release, I noticed his holoscreen sitting out on a shelf, as plain as day, and just waiting for me to take it. He kissed me, hard enough that I tasted my own blood in my mouth as his teeth scraped against my lips, and no longer seemed concerned with my body's lack of a response, which was good because I'd barely grown hard. In Asiq I could easily pretend; here none of my usual tricks had worked. Not even thinking about Emmanuel's naked back under my hands, his hard, firm butt against me. It was a fantasy, not that I thought I'd ever actually get to have him. No, that wasn't going to happen. But I'd hoped it would work while Mr. Diab had fussed at me. Eventually he'd stopped caring about a minor detail like whether or not I was hard and had simply taken me as he wanted to.

He got off the bed and gave my butt a hard squeeze. If I didn't already have purple skin, I would have likely bruised from his treatment. "I'm going to shower," he said, moving away from me. "I expect you to be here, right like this, when I get back."

I smiled at him over my shoulder and gave him a wink. "Of course I will be." He'd kidnapped me, and I had no way off his ship. Where else was I supposed to go? I blew him a kiss.

"You are so beautiful. We will have so much fun together."

Yes, so much fun, as I watched Emmanuel kill him. That would be highly entertaining for me. Wherever this new bloodthirsty streak had come from, I hoped it hung around long enough for me to enjoy Mr. Diab's death. "See you soon."

He was out of the room a few minutes later, and I waited for him to get into the shower, the door closing loudly behind him, before I got up and went to his holoscreen. I had a moment of panic as I wondered if he might have locked it, like I kept mine locked, but he wasn't that worried about security apparently, because I was easily able to get to his messaging system.

> *Emmanuel—*
> *Kidnapped. Embedding the coordinates in this message. Starting a distress signal too. Get me out of here. I'll pay you to kill the person that ordered me taken. Not my holoscreen. Don't reply. And don't tell Monroe.*
> *—Corbin*

There. I thought that was sufficiently good enough to get his attention. I deleted the message after I'd sent it, making sure there was no trace of it. The distress signal was trickier, but I'd played a prank on Thierry once on his own holoscreen where I'd done a nearly invisible tracker, and the station's security had kept asking him what his emergency was for nearly a month. He'd been pretty fed up after a while, and so had they. I employed the same trick now, then put Mr. Diab's holoscreen back exactly as I'd found it.

Getting back into the same position I had been was a bit trickier, as I'd only wanted to get off the bed and to the holoscreen a few minutes before. Maneuvering a little, I figured I finally got it right because as soon as Mr. Diab came out of the shower, he grinned at me. Thinking about how very much Emmanuel was going to make him pay made me happy too, and the smile I gave him in return was completely genuine, though for an entirely different reason than his.

CHAPTER
TEN

DINNER CAME next for me, which was a gelatinous mix of different colored space-travel-ready sludges that provided nutrition but not much else. I ate it because I had to, and because I was mildly hungry, but mostly because I didn't want to upset my captor as he watched me with a smile.

"Once we get to my home planet, you'll have all the food you could want," he promised me.

I nodded. I'd assumed Mr. Diab didn't eat like this normally, but right then I desperately missed the rich cured meats and soft cheeses, not to mention all the chocolate I could possibly eat, that I got on Asiq. I pretended to like the disgusting food, all the while hoping my brother didn't have to survive on it while he was out in space, before I felt like I could pretend to be no longer hungry without insulting him.

"Thank you for the meal," I told Mr. Diab. He had his men around us—three guards—and I'd done my best to ignore them. I was pretty sure, since they worked for Mr. Diab, that they wouldn't be of any help to me, but I was also a bit annoyed at their continued attention. I wasn't some attraction for them to stare at, and being treated as such was getting old quite quickly.

One of them reached for me, and I jerked my arm away from his fingers before he could touch me. But when I looked up at Mr. Diab, I saw that the gesture hadn't gone unnoticed, and he was glaring at his guard. Without a word he took out his neutralizer and shot him in the chest. As he writhed on the floor, I turned away, unwilling to see him go through pain. He'd wanted to touch me, which I didn't appreciate, but that was nothing new. Being held by someone willing to cause pain to their guard for something so small was completely alien to me, and I had a hard time coming back to being normal after that.

"Corbin is not to be touched," Mr. Diab announced.

When he looked at me like he expected something from me, I knew I had to give him something. I forced out my best smile and reached across the small, steel table to touch him on his wrist even as I wanted to recoil from him. "Thank you. I feel truly safe and protected with you around." Normally I was fine with lying, with pretending in general. With Mr. Diab, however, it was getting harder and harder for me to be anything but disgusted with him.

He took my hand and led me from the table, making me step over the man whose frozen face was still wrought with pain. I tried not to look and failed miserably, but maybe my reaction to his ordeal didn't show on my face.

It must not have, because a second later Mr. Diab took me into his arms, and a guard turned on a slow sort of music, something I didn't recognize, but the tone was familiar enough. I laid my head on his shoulder and put my hands over his arms, as I was expected to do when I danced with a client. But I desperately wanted to go home.

"No one here will hurt you," he promised me, his voice an icy chill against the side of my neck.

No one, except for him of course. "Thank you."

He kissed the side of my neck, which would have usually elicited some sort of a reaction from me, so I forced myself to sigh, loudly, as if in pleasure. I felt worn out, on edge, and as if my mask was beginning to crack. I could only pretend for so long, and my record with a client had been four hours. And I'd been having fun the whole time. This was a miserable sort of torture, and I knew I couldn't keep it up.

Thankfully I didn't have to, as no more than ten minutes later, Mr. Diab released me, gave me a kiss on my cheek, and stepped back. "You're likely tired, Corbin. It's been a long day for you. I'd like you to go get some rest. Come, I'll show you where."

I was relieved and glad when one of the guards brought me to quarters I hoped would be all mine. But that was not to be the case, as I recognized Mr. Diab's quarters from before.

"If you need anything, let us know. We are here to serve him," the guard said solemnly as if it was some sort of vow, more than a contract he'd taken on, that made him stay with Mr. Diab. Whatever the case was, I had no interest in finding out more about him or anyone else on this ship. I simply wanted off.

I gave him a tight nod. "Thank you. I think I'll be fine." Manners still counted, even to the guards, especially while I wanted to curse at him and everyone else inside the shiny metal hull.

"Good night, then."

He closed the hatch behind himself, and I heard it click into place. Mr. Diab may have wanted me around, but he'd also locked me in, clearly not trusting me simply to stay put. With a heavy groan, I lay back on the bed and waited for my captor to come back to bother me some more.

It took hours, not that I would have complained about Mr. Diab's absence, and in that time I thought about my brother and how I was glad he didn't know I'd been kidnapped because I didn't want him worrying about me when I knew I would be just fine as soon as Emmanuel came for me.

And I thought about Monroe and how I'd never really told him it was okay that he was in love with my brother but how I'd given Thierry such a hard time, not just about Monroe owning a brothel, but because of their age difference. I wasn't entirely sure just how old Monroe was, but I knew he was at least twenty years older than my brother was. That had bothered me a lot when they'd first gotten together.

It was one thing to have sex with someone double my age. I'd done that plenty of times, but falling in love with him was a completely different scenario. As I lay there in Mr. Diab's bed, I wished that I could go back and be more supportive of their relationship when it had first been starting out. Maybe then Thierry wouldn't have kept so much from me.

He still might have, simply because neither of us had known how I'd react to hearing that he had fallen for Monroe, and he'd kept a lot of secrets from me for months. But I wondered, if my reaction had been different, if he wouldn't have done that. It didn't matter now, of course, but that's what I thought about while I lay in the unfamiliar bed and waited for my captor to come back for me.

Waiting was the worst part by far, while I lay there unsure of what Mr. Diab had in store for me. He'd use me, that was a given, but it was the rest of it that worried me. I should have tried to sleep, but my brain refused to shut off. Instead I lay there, with the minutes counting down, as I drummed my fingers over my stomach and looked up at the steel ceiling.

CHAPTER
ELEVEN

TWO DAYS later while I sat in the dining area with Mr. Diab across from me, eating green sludge for breakfast, the ship shook with what sounded like an explosion, and my sour mood instantly picked up.

"Find out what that was!" Mr. Diab barked at the guards keeping watch around us. He reached across the table to rest his hand on my wrist. For the first time since being kidnapped, I didn't have to keep myself from recoiling. I even managed a real smile for him because the explosion, I was sure, meant that Emmanuel was coming to get me out of there.

"You're safe. I'll make sure of it. No one will hurt you here," Mr. Diab told me again. I was so sick of hearing those words from him, but I bit down on my tongue.

"Boss!" one of the guards called, and Mr. Diab left to go see what was happening. I sat right where I was, not wanting to get in Emmanuel's way.

But it wasn't Emmanuel who came crashing through the hatch a few minutes later. This man was Sythe, like me, and he pointed a gun at me, a real one, not a neutralizer. I froze, not even able to breathe, until he lowered his arm. And then he did the strangest thing. He simply smiled at me.

"Corbin?"

I nodded to him. Did he want to kill me? Was this another bounty hunter the senator had hired to silence me, assuming I had tried to reveal his secrets, which I had not?

He offered me his hand, and I stared at it for a moment. "Come on. Em sent me. I'm Resan." I didn't take his hand, not at first. "Or do you want to stay here?"

"Absolutely not." I got up without touching him. As Sythe, he would likely be just as reactive as I was. And I didn't want to set him off, or myself, when I really needed to get out of there. He led the way out of the room, and I stayed close behind him. He didn't ask me if I needed to grab anything before we left, not that I did. I'd been taken in my sleep. There was nothing I would have been able to grab.

As soon as we got to the bridge, and why we were going there was completely beyond me since I figured that would be where Mr. Diab likely was, people started shooting at us. And they weren't using neutralizers either.

Resan pushed me down behind a solid steel wall, protecting me, and I turned to look up at him as he fired off round after round of hot laser energy. He was hit in the leg, but he only grimaced, and I wondered at a Sythe, with our ability to feel everything physical so much more explosively than everyone else, being a bounty hunter. If that's what Resan was. By the concentration on his face and the tight line of his mouth, I was sure he had shut himself down. I'd been shut down as much as I could be since being kidnapped, and it hurt to do so for too long. We were naturally open, experiencing the world of touch with such blinding, beautiful brilliance, and I didn't want him to have to suffer as he continued to shoot at Mr. Diab and his men.

I reached out and wrapped my fingers around Resan's ankle. I felt the heat of his skin the moment he allowed himself to feel my touch, and his face softened.

The shooting slowed until it stopped, leaving only the silence of our heavy breathing. He gave me a nod, and I released my fingers from his skin.

"Thank you for that."

Nodding, I got to my feet. "Are you hurt badly?"

"No. I've had far worse."

I looked around the corner and cringed. I'd wanted Mr. Diab to be hurt, but Resan had destroyed him, leaving very little of the man to be recognized. I quickly looked away.

"Do you want to stay here until Emmanuel comes, or would you rather spend the time in my shuttle? It isn't as big—"

"Is it free of dead bodies?" I asked, interrupting him.

He laughed. "Yes."

"Then I'd rather be there."

We had to go through the blood and gore to get to his shuttle, and I held my breath, wishing I didn't have to see the bodies riddled with large seeping holes, but if I'd closed my eyes, I would have likely fallen into one of them.

"No stomach for it?" he asked as we approached the airlock to the shuttle dock. We were lucky Mr. Diab's ship had been large enough to have a docking port. Not all ships did, and I didn't want to have to take the time to find a suit. All I wanted was to be off the ship with its dead bodies and bloodstained bridge.

"I doubt many people do." His shuttle was barely larger than mine, currently docked back at my home station. But it was comfortable, and he'd kept it warmed up, likely for a quick takeoff. I found a seat and strapped myself in as he released us from the dock and began easing us out of the asteroid belt.

We weren't too far out into open space when he stalled us out and came to sit across from me in the passenger hold of the shuttle. "Emmanuel should be here by tomorrow. He had something to take care of."

"Killing someone?" I asked him bluntly.

He looked surprised at my directness, but why he was, I couldn't imagine. I'd just seen him shoot and kill people, and I knew Emmanuel was a bounty hunter too. Resan nodded, and I relaxed into the back of my seat as the warmth of his shuttle started to work through me. I was able to breathe normally for the first time in days, and I hadn't worried about the senator sending someone to kill me until Resan had shown up.

"You can sleep now, if you want to," Resan offered me as he began cutting the leg of his pants away to treat his wound. I saw that it was little more than a graze and had stopped bleeding, before looking away from him.

"Thank you." Without having to be on edge all the time and feel like I had to play a part for Mr. Diab, I suddenly did feel tired. But I had questions for him first. "How are you able to be a bounty hunter when you're Sythe?"

"Two things," he replied with a smile as he finished bandaging his leg up. "I'm a peacekeeper, not a bounty hunter. And I'm only half Sythe. My other half is Pulden. I still react, like you do, and I can shut myself down or open myself up, like my mother can. But I have the resiliency and strength of a Pulden."

"And the reflexes," I guessed as well, remembering how good he had been in the bridge.

He gave me a little nod. "Perfect combination for peacekeeping."

I supposed that a peacekeeper working with a bounty hunter wasn't too strange. It wasn't as if either of them were doing anything illegal, though bounty hunters did skirt that line quite frequently. Their work was regulated, but not so much so that people couldn't get through the cracks anyway.

"How did you and Emmanuel meet?" He'd referred to him as "Em," something I found endearing, but it wasn't a name I'd be using with him.

"Em recruited me, actually. I was trained by him as a bounty hunter after he saw me fighting in a bar years ago. I decided collecting bounties wasn't for me, but I did enjoy the fighting, the shooting, and the having something to do and stand for besides my own ego. Peacekeeping seemed like the perfect place for me, and I fit in well at the peacekeepers guild. With Em's training I was quickly recognized for my talents."

He sounded so proud of himself and quite infatuated with Emmanuel. I wasn't jealous, and the realization they'd likely had, and may have even continued to have, a close relationship didn't bother me in the least. I was attracted to Emmanuel, we'd kissed and more, but he wasn't mine to lay claim to in any way.

"How did you meet him?" Resan asked.

I was growing steadily more tired by the moment, and I found it hard to keep my eyes open for much longer as I started to drift off in the peace and warmth of his shuttle. "I was one of his bounties."

Resan snorted. "You're lucky to be alive right now, then, and even luckier that he sent someone after you when you put out that distress call."

I knew I was. "I'm sure it's simply the credits I pay him not to kill me."

Resan didn't look so sure, though. "He chooses who he takes out or lets live with a lot more concern than simply for credits. Why was he ordered to kill you anyway?"

Sleep rushed toward me like a comet. "I'm an aspasian. A client wanted me dead." With a sigh I closed my eyes and let myself be taken by the darkness of a dreamless sleep.

CHAPTER
TWELVE

WHEN I woke up, I heard Emmanuel's voice. Immediately after realizing that, I also noticed how I was lying on the floor, and a jacket had been wrapped up and put under my head. An emergency blanket was tucked in around me, and I smiled as I thought about either Resan or Emmanuel taking the time to make me comfortable as I slept. It was slightly disturbing that I hadn't noticed someone moving me, but I didn't put too much thought into it as I slowly sat up and looked toward the control panel where I could see Resan and Emmanuel sitting together and talking quietly.

I stretched my arms in front of myself and wished I had something to wear other than the sleep pants I'd been in the past few days. I'd been allowed to shower, but Mr. Diab had told me if I wanted to wear something besides the pants I'd been taken in, my only other option was to be naked. That hadn't been something I'd been willing to do. Thankfully he'd taken my excuse of being shy around his men as my reason for not agreeing to such a ridiculous thing.

Now I stood, lifting the jacket I knew was Emmanuel's with me. I put it on, zipped it up to my chin, and couldn't help breathing him in. It was impossible to sneak up on the two of them, but I tried to be quiet anyway as I approached them and found a seat behind Resan so that I could watch Emmanuel.

"Hello," he said to me.

I nodded to him. "Thank you for sending Resan to come get me."

"Were you hurt while you were being held?"

That was a loaded question, depending on his definition of "hurt." I considered lying to him, but he'd gone through the trouble of sending his friend out to rescue me, and Resan had been shot at in the process. I figured he'd earned my honesty in this regard. "I was used but otherwise untouched."

He pulled his mouth down into a dark frown and shook his head. "I'm sorry I wasn't there to protect you."

His remorse wasn't needed. "I was at home when I was taken. I should have been safe there. I believed, clearly incorrectly, that no one from Asiq knew where I lived. Mr. Diab must have followed me or had someone follow me for him." It was the only thing that made sense to me.

"Resan is taking us to your station now. I'll stay with you for a few days, to make sure you're safe, then I will leave you," Emmanuel said. There was such finality in his words, as if that was the last time I would ever see him, that it had me frowning at him.

"Don't I still need to be saved from Senator Saunders?" I asked.

Resan turned in his seat and looked between us. "Isn't that the name of the senator that just died? Heart attack, wasn't it?"

No, that was too convenient. I looked to Emmanuel for confirmation. He gave me a quick nod. "How did you manage to make him die of a heart attack?"

Resan turned away from us. "This isn't something I particularly need to know about. Unless he was a criminal?" he asked, sounding hopeful.

"Nothing confirmed," Emmanuel replied.

Resan shook his head. "Then I don't want to know."

I smiled at Emmanuel. "Thank you."

He reached over and touched my knee. So, I'd only get a few more days with him. We weren't exceptionally close by any means, so that prospect shouldn't have bothered me as much as it did. I shouldn't have wanted more time with him. I shouldn't have wondered what he'd do after he left my apartment. I probably shouldn't have cared.

And yet I did.

Two days later Resan dropped us off, and Emmanuel docked his shuttle outside my front door. It was good to be home, and I showered and changed instantly. It would be good to be back on Asiq in a few days, back where there was good food and actual water for my showers. When I came out, Emmanuel was ready to go in.

"May I?"

"It's just steam," I told him. It was better than nothing, but it wasn't the kind of clean I felt like I needed.

"That's fine."

I stepped aside to give him room. "Then it's all yours."

No more than ten minutes later, he was done and changed into yet another black outfit. He joined me on the couch, though there were other places to sit in the small living room, and I found myself moving toward him as if I was drawn somehow.

"Thank you again for sending Resan out to get me."

He put his arm around my shoulders, then moved his hand to the back of the couch instead as if touching me was somehow not okay. "I'm sorry I couldn't do it myself. I was too far away, and I wanted you safe sooner, rather than having to wait for me to get there."

I understood that, absolutely. And I appreciated his concern.

"Were you afraid with him?" Emmanuel asked.

"Maybe… at first. But mostly I was simply angry at him and his nerve at taking me in the first place." With him so close, I knew that I didn't want him to go. A few days wouldn't be enough. I wanted him to hang around for a while.

I turned on the couch and ran my fingers from his neck and down the front of his shirt where it was exposed between his open jacket lapels. When he turned to look at me, maybe to ask me what I was doing, I instead kissed him.

I'd been open when we'd been on Resan's ship, but neither of them had touched me much. Now it was as if I practically needed his warmth, his touch, on me as I slid myself onto his lap. He gripped my hips, holding me tightly, as I flared to life on top of him.

He slipped his tongue between my lips, and I groaned into his open mouth. But far too soon, he stopped us, tossing me onto my back on the couch beside him, and worse, not following along on top of me like he should have been doing. "You don't owe me this. Or anything else. You paid me to protect you, and I was simply following through."

That's what he thought I'd been doing? I glared at him for his stupidity. "I was kissing you because I wanted to."

He clearly didn't believe me as he shook his head. "Why would you? You wouldn't. Of course not. You were kidnapped. And forced to have sex with him."

Sighing, I shook my head. I wanted to kiss him because I found pleasure in the experience, and his insistence that I somehow had no idea of what I was doing bothered me. "You're frustrating."

"So are you," he said with a smirk.

That made me laugh. "Let me kiss you, then."

"I wouldn't want to stop at only a kiss," he quietly admitted, his gaze locked with mine.

I nodded, understanding him completely. "I don't want to either. And I am myself right now, whether you believe me or not." That seemed to be enough for him as I slid between his knees to kneel on the floor.

I enjoyed giving people pleasure, whether it was making them laugh with a joke, or giving them oral as I intended to do with Emmanuel. He, on the other hand, didn't look nearly as sure of himself as I felt, as I ran my hands over his inner thighs, coming near the zipper of his pants but not quite going there. Not yet at least. I wanted to tease him a little first.

He reached down to grab me, and I arched up into his rough kiss as he circled his hand around my neck then moved on to wrap my hair around his hand. I hissed into his mouth when he gave my hair a hard tug, pulling my head back and separating our lips.

"I shouldn't want you as much as I do," he told me as he released my hair and dragged his fingertips over my cheek before pulling away from me completely to rest his hand back on his thigh.

"And I shouldn't want a bounty hunter who tried to shoot me with a neutralizer the first time we met. Yet here we are." I tried not to snap at him, but I was getting tired of this with him. If he wanted me, fine. If he didn't because of who I was and what I did, that was on him. I wanted to enjoy him and give him pleasure.

Emmanuel gave me a soft smile and brought his hand back to my face. I flared open for him and sighed at the feel of his rough fingertips against my cheek. He ran his thumb over my bottom lip, and I sucked the pad of his finger between my teeth, getting a bigger smile from him.

"Let me," I told him, releasing his thumb as I ran my hand lightly down the front of his pants. "I want to."

He nodded, silently giving me his permission, as he laid his head back. Emmanuel kept his hand on my face as I opened his pants, but I would have rather had him watching me. I would have enjoyed it more. As it was, I still took my time slowly stroking him, giving him every bit of pleasure that I could as I heard his soft moans rise.

He was thick and beautiful, the silver of his skin extending even to his swollen tip, which I eagerly took into my mouth. It was my turn to moan as I tasted him, enjoying him for myself. With clients, I used my mouth to give them pleasure all the time. But we were in my apartment, and Emmanuel wasn't a client. It had been at least a year since I'd had sex outside Asiq, and I realized that I'd missed the intimacy of it, the having someone here in a space that had become just mine after my brother had taken his first internship, the being open with someone as much as having them here made me be.

I took him to his base and held myself there as I listened to low noises, letting me know he was enjoying every second of this. I wanted more for him, absolutely, but this was a good way to start and get him to relax some. He was still so tightly wound, as if he expected trouble at every turn. And maybe I should have been the same way as him, alert and on edge, ready to fight as he seemed to be. It seemed too easy to me that he'd been able to kill the senator while Resan killed Mr. Diab, and now I was free on both sides.

But that was a worry for another day and another time. The only person I wanted to focus on right then was Emmanuel and making sure he got everything he wanted from me, and in turn that I had everything from him as well.

I lifted my mouth up, ready to slide off him, but he moved his hand to the back of my head, holding me there for a little while longer. I looked up at him to find him watching me too and slowly allowed him to control me. This wasn't something I did too often, even with clients I had known for months, because it put me in such a delicate and vulnerable position. But I didn't stop him. I simply tasted him and ran my tongue over him as he gently eased my lips over his shaft.

After a few more minutes, he let me go, and I silently got to my feet. I reached out my hand to him, which he took, and I pulled him into my bedroom. I hadn't expected guests, and my bed had been left a mess since my kidnapping, but I made him focus on me and not those details as I pulled him down on top of me.

"How do you want me?" I whispered huskily to him as I began pulling off his clothes.

He roughly kissed me, crashing his lips against mine as soon as I had his shirt off and could feel him rubbing against me. "For myself," he said, pushing my face aside so that he could kiss my neck. I didn't mind that he wanted to be forceful with me, to show me how much stronger than me he was. It was actually a turn-on, and I easily went with it as he sucked on my skin and ran his hands down my chest to settle on my pants.

Between the two of us, I was naked under him in no time at all, and I lay there watching his reaction as he looked me over, then quickly followed his hand as he lay on his side and stroked his fingers down my exposed skin.

"You're beautiful," he told me.

I was used to hearing that, but it still made me happy that he thought so. It was good to get compliments from someone I wanted as much in that moment as I wanted him. His pants came off quickly under my expert touch, and I was glad to see he didn't try to hide himself from me as we lay there together, looking at each other in the harsh light of my bedroom.

CHAPTER
THIRTEEN

"WHY ARE you so tense?" I asked him.

Emmanuel smiled at me and dragged the knuckles of his right hand down my sternum, ending his path just before my navel. "Why are you?"

I smirked and quickly shook my head. "No, we won't be doing that game. I ask you a question, and you answer."

"Only if I get the same from you."

That was easy enough. "Fine. Answer my question first." Before he could, though, I propped myself up on my elbows and leaned forward to kiss him along his chin. He turned his face to kiss me too, and I lay back as he slid on top of me.

"I don't do this often," he told me between kisses.

"Have sex with aspasians?" I guessed as I ran my hands over his wide shoulders. I loved how built he was, how he made even me, with my well-taken-care-of body, seem somehow delicate. I could be lithe, and I had been called graceful before, but it wasn't a normal part of being me. When I was at home and alone, I was clumsy sometimes, and I ran into things. I was sometimes lazy and just put my hair in a braid instead of combing it out, and I usually didn't eat very well.

He chuckled, and I felt the sound come through my chest since he was on top of me. "No. Be intimate with anyone. It isn't part of being a bounty hunter, and I have little time for anything else. Now why are you tense?"

I answered him while I mulled over what he'd said. "I'm really not, but if I am at all it's because I haven't had anyone here with me in over a year. My needs are met at Asiq." I didn't understand not having time for sex, but that was really much of my life while I was at work, so maybe that explained why I was having trouble with what he'd said. It didn't make a lot of sense to me, but I didn't question it either. There was no reason to when I could tell easily enough that he was stating the truth by the gentle tremble of his shoulders I could feel under my fingertips.

"So this is different for both of us." He sounded relieved at that.

"It is. Is there anything you particularly want? Me to call you something? My nails running down your back?"

He brought his mouth back to my neck, gently nuzzling me between kisses. "Em. You can call me Em. For tonight."

I nodded and ran my hands down his back. "Em. I like that." He brought one of his hands to the underside of my knee and pushed me back. I brought my other leg around his hip, getting ready for him.

My nerves were already humming from allowing myself to be open, and when I felt him pushing against me, it felt like fire. I braced myself for the pain, since he hadn't stretched me at all, and I wondered why I didn't say anything to him about it. Maybe I was so used to not asking my clients for things that I couldn't even tell someone what I needed in my own apartment. That was a chilling thought.

Before I could dwell too long on it, though, he seemed to come back to remembering that there were things that had to be done first, and I felt him stretching me. There was still burning and a rough pain that made me cringe as he pushed his way into my body, despite his preparations.

He hissed against my collarbone as he rested his forehead against me. He strokes were jerky, giving me even more evidence that he didn't have sex often, and I closed my eyes, wishing I'd done this my way.

Only, it wasn't too late to get what I needed from him so that we could both experience this the right way, I realized. "Em. Stop for a second."

"Is this wrong?" he asked me, stopping instantly.

I shook my head. Someone he'd been with at some point may have liked things like that, but I wasn't that person, and I wanted to enjoy this too, instead of treating him like a client who could enjoy me however they pleased.

"No. But I have another idea. Let me up?"

I kept my tone casual, not letting him know I hadn't been enjoying having him in me. Instead, when he moved back, I smiled at him, gave him a quick kiss on his nose, then went to my dresser where I kept some of the small packages of lubricant Monroe handed out like the chocolate candies in Asiq.

Emmanuel looked uncomfortable as I moved him onto his back and got above him. "Relax," I told him, giving him a kiss. He wrapped his arms around my shoulders, holding me tightly, as we continued to kiss.

While I slipped my tongue into his mouth and felt his hands curling into my long hair, I moved one hand behind myself and began stroking him with the lube, getting him nice and slick for me. He groaned into my mouth, seeming surprised as I brought him back to my entrance and slowly took him inside at the speed I was comfortable with. He had no control this way, but he didn't seem to mind that as I kept kissing him.

It took longer for him to get inside me this time, but once I had him in and I pulled back so that I could slide onto his base, I saw the appreciation in his expression. This was a man used to taking control, but sex was my world, and I knew what worked.

"Better?" I asked him, perhaps a bit smugly, as I ran my hands down his chest. My movements on top of him were small, enough to give us both pleasure, but not so much that I was bouncing all around like I was on a giant inflatable ball.

He nodded to me and covered my hand with his. "I'm sorry I did it wrong."

Shrugging, I brushed off his apology. "You didn't. I just prefer things a different way."

It was slow, the barest movements of my body over his as I felt a flush come over my purple skin. I saw him darken with color as well as a faint blush of pink formed under the silver of his own skin.

I flared for him, and also myself, enjoying every second of having him in me as I rocked over him and felt him touch the best parts of me. He

85

settled his hands loosely on my hips, barely touching me. When I rocked forward, though, and ran my nails lightly over his chest, he tightened his fingers over my skin. I smiled at him, knowing he wanted to be rougher with me. Maybe he even wanted to try to control me, if only for tonight. "I'm not that delicate, Em. You can squeeze me." I put my hands over his fingers on my hip, telling him exactly what I was hinting at.

"I don't want to hurt you," he quietly protested.

That was sweet, and I was glad he didn't intend to do any real damage to me that night. But really, his concern wasn't necessary. "I'm an aspasian and have been doing this about half my life. I've got decades of being with different people under my nonexistent belt. You're not going to hurt me unless you whip out an invisible neutralizer. I trust you. Consider trusting yourself. Just tonight?"

He blushed and chewed on his bottom lip for a moment. I waited, wondering at how a man who had wanted to kill me only a short time ago could look so unsure of himself and so vulnerable. It shouldn't have been possible, but as he made his decision and tightened his fingers on my hips hard enough to leave bruises on me the next morning, I couldn't help wanting to protect him, as silly a thought as that was.

"Is that okay?"

"I wouldn't let you do it if it wasn't."

He frowned at me and tried to loosen his hands, but I shook my head, stopping him before he could pull away and try to change his mind. "You're smaller than me. You wouldn't be able to stop me from hurting you if I wanted to."

Was that what he was so afraid of? I sighed and went still on top of his lap so that I could lean forward and brace one hand on the mattress next to his shoulder and the other on his chest, right over his heart. "Em, you're not going to hurt me. At all. I'm not fragile, and I'm not some virgin you need to be careful with. You can have sex with me like you mean it. Like you want to. Stop holding back. I'll be fine."

He still didn't look convinced, so I moved my hand that had been over his heart to his silvery nipple. With my thumbnail I scratched lightly

86

at that tight bundle of nerves. He gasped, and I smiled, knowing he liked that as much as I did. No longer interested in simply teasing him, I twisted his nipple between my thumb and finger. Em arched off the bed, and I grinned down at him. He pushed me back down on his cock with his hands firmly planted on my hips, and I leaned back, not releasing his nipple. Instead I took up toying with the other one and watched his face as I eased myself over his cock and played with his nipples.

He moved toward me, telling me without a single word that he enjoyed every second of my play. "That's good, Em. Show me what you like." I kept one hand on his left nipple, but my right hand I slid down his ribs, letting my nails drag over his skin hard enough to leave light pink scratches in my wake. He hissed and closed his eyes. Leaning forward, I licked down his neck. He moved his hands from my hips to my shoulders, holding me tightly against him. I didn't mind.

Rolling me over so that he was back on top of me took skill to do right, which he didn't have enough experience to master, but he didn't muck it up too badly at least. He hovered above me, as if waiting for me to tell him he'd done something right, but I didn't need to tell him that. I kissed him instead. My normal bed partners were far more confident than he was, which was refreshing in itself. That he seemed to think I was capable of being broken by sex, though, was beginning to grate on my nerves.

I hooked my legs behind him, pulling him into me from the back of his thighs. "Harder," I told him, hoping the sternness of my voice let him know exactly what I wanted from him. No delicacy, no games. Just him giving me everything he could and then some.

"I don't want to hurt—"

I pursed my lips and tried very hard to find some patience. "Have you ever had sex with someone you weren't afraid of damaging somehow? Someone you didn't see as a victim that you just had to save from being kidnapped?"

He nodded. "Of course I have. Being a bounty hunter, I don't go around saving people that often. I'm much more in the bagging and killing business."

Against all logic that made me laugh, and I nipped lightly at his chin. "Then treat me like them. How are you with those people you don't feel the need to worry over?"

"Are you sure?"

Absolutely. I was very sure. If I had been any more sure, I would be begging him. I was still in the talking phase, though, where I was trying to reason with him and get him to see some form of logic before I went mad with frustration over his stubbornness.

Very slowly, as if he was sure I was going to change my mind at any second and tell him to get off me, he brought first one of my hands, then the other, above my head to rest on the pillow. "Don't move them from there."

"Or what?" I asked him with a smirk, already liking this game.

He leaned down and lightly kissed me on my forehead. It was an incredibly chaste kiss for a man who had his cock buried to the hilt in my ass. "Or I won't let you come." He seemed unsure of himself, as if he didn't know if he could actually stop me. That wouldn't do.

I dropped my voice, and my chin. "Yes, sir." Submitting for a game was easy for me. I did it all the time with a bunch of different clients. Whatever game he wanted to play, I was able to do that without a second thought.

Saying that, though, must have been wrong because he froze above me. I looked up to see him staring down at me. "No, not that. Don't say that."

"Okay. I won't. Want to tell me why?"

Em relaxed, just slightly, above me. "When I take a job, when I'm asked to go kill someone, every master I've ever had has insisted I call them that. And I don't want that word here. Not with you and not between us."

I understood that perfectly. I was calling him that for a game anyway, not as a real form of submission. "Of course." Not moving my hands at all, I leaned up and kissed him gently on his neck. Then I ran my tongue down his neck until I was able to kiss his collarbone.

He was slow when he started, as if he was still afraid of hurting me with each thrust. I bit him on his collarbone in my annoyance, hoping he got the message loud and clear that I wasn't interested in going slow.

As I sank my teeth into his skin, his movements became jerky. That lack of control was exactly what I'd been hoping for, and I eagerly welcomed his thrusts into my body until he found a rhythm he liked that had him forcing me deep into the mattress. He leaned over me, covering my body with his bigger one, and I felt completely enclosed. Instead of being trapped, as I'd sometimes felt with my clients, I felt perfectly secure with my Em-shaped shield.

Tightening my legs over his hips and digging my left heel into his butt cheek, I was able to get him to go even deeper. I didn't try to hide my groan, or the gasps that came past my lips as each thrust rubbed him against my cock.

"Em!" I gasped as he rubbed hard against me, sending thrilling waves of pleasure straight through my cock and out to every other heightened nerve on my body.

"Are you okay? Should I stop?"

"I might end up killing you if you did," I snapped at him. Taking a breath was hard, but I managed it. "If you were serious about not letting me come until you wanted me to, you might want to let me soon."

He looked confused for a second. "I didn't mean to say that. I just meant that I wasn't going to let you if you moved your hands. Are you ready?"

I felt ridiculous for not understanding what he said, but since he wasn't going to deny me my pleasure, I saw no reason to worry about it as I nodded to him. When I'd said his name, he'd pulled up a little, giving me enough room to ease my hand between us. But he covered my wrist with his hand and shook his head at me, stopping me from getting myself off.

I was disappointed, but only for a moment, until I saw him put his own hand between us, and a second later, I felt his fist around my shaft. I smiled up at him and closed my eyes as he began thrusting into me again.

"Look at me, Corbin."

That was the kind of command I wasn't used to hearing. Most people didn't care if I came or if I was looking at them when they did. But I turned my head to look at him all the same. He kissed me, then left his mouth only an inch above mine as he stroked me hard and fast, being rough with me as I writhed under him. With him so close, he had to hear every gasp, every low groan that came out of my lips. And there was no hiding from him as he watched me. My pleasure couldn't be faked from this close, there was only honesty between us, and it was beautiful.

As the first wave of pleasure hit me full force, I dug my fingers hard into his shoulders, half sure I drew blood with my fingernails. He didn't seem to notice, or care, as he kept stroking me. I felt wet heat spray against my stomach and knew that, as close as he was to me, he hadn't been able to escape my come either. Em didn't seem to mind, though, as he slowly released me. Another kiss later and he was back to thrusting inside me. There was a speed, an intensity to his movements now, as if he desperately needed the kind of pleasure I was basking in. I could barely keep my eyes open, but I forced myself to so that I could see his face the moment his orgasm came over him as well.

I wasn't disappointed as he cried out and spilled inside me. He fell over me, laying his forehead against my neck. He whispered my name, and I smiled as we lay together, both of us in no hurry to move as we clung to the pleasure we'd brought each other.

CHAPTER
FOURTEEN

THE NEXT morning, I left him in bed while I went to shower. Still naked, he was stunning as he lay over my crumpled sheets. It was a shame to leave him, but I needed to get ready. When I came back out, pulling up my pants as I walked out of the bathroom, he was sitting up on the edge of the bed.

Em offered me his hand, and I reached for him too. I found myself being pulled onto his lap, and I smiled at him as I sat down over his thighs. "Come back to bed," he said.

Not that I didn't want to join him in where his mind was already going, but I had things to do. "Wish I could, but I need to get ready."

His hands on my hips stilled. "For what?"

"It's been two weeks. I'm expected back at Asiq today...." I wasn't surprised that he didn't remember how long it had been since I was just at work, but I didn't expect how his expression hardened by the second.

Em roughly pushed me away, and I stumbled on the hem of my pants as I fell off his lap, but I didn't fall to the floor. As soon as I straightened up, I crossed my arms over my chest and stared him down. He looked just as angry as I imagined I did, as he looked right back at me.

"You're not going back there," he told me, his voice hard. It made him sound dangerous. Too bad for him I wasn't in the least bit afraid of him, especially not after seeing how vulnerable and unsure of himself he'd been with me the night before. It was almost funny that he thought he had any right to order me about, like he had some claim to me or what I did with my life when he'd barely begun to be a part of it.

I raised an eyebrow. "And why not?"

Apparently he didn't like me looming over him because he got to his feet as well. Naked and angry, he looked nearly feral as he stared down at me. "Because you were just kidnapped. Because killing Saunders and Diab was too easy. Someone else could still come after you."

He was right; I could still be in danger, but that didn't mean I was going to stop living my life on my own terms. "You're going to have to do better than that if you expect me not to go to work today. And what's your alternative anyway? I stay with you where you can keep me safe forever?" The idea was laughable. He was a bounty hunter; being safe wasn't exactly part of his job either. I moved past him so that I could pull a shirt out of my closet and finish getting dressed. He stood there stubbornly as if staring at the back of my head was going to change anything.

"What would get you to give it up?"

"Being an aspasian?" I guessed as I turned to look at him over my shoulder while I pulled a shirt off a hanger. He gave me a single nod, as if he wasn't quite sure why he was asking me that. Which was good, because it made two of us then that were confused by his question. "Nothing," I told him honestly. He looked as if he didn't believe me, so I turned around to face him while I pulled a tight shirt over my head. I was back in work mode, back to choosing what I wore because I knew what looked good on me, what would make men want me, more than what I was comfortable sitting around on my ass in. "I've never wanted to give it up. I have no intention of not being an aspasian. Until the day Monroe tells me I'm too old to work for him and that I need to get my wrinkly ass out of his brothel, I will still be working there."

For some reason Em actually looked hurt by my words, though I couldn't imagine why. "You don't have to worry about me while I'm there. Monroe can protect me."

"He wasn't able to stop me from getting to you."

I ignored his entirely truthful and incredibly unhelpful reminder. "You're special. You know that. All badass bounty hunter." I gave him a smile, which he didn't return, so I quickly dropped it. "And if you want last night to happen again, you're welcome at Asiq. Or you can come back here and visit me on my weeks off. I'd let you in."

"I don't want to pay you for sex." He bit the words out as if they tasted disgusting in his mouth. I couldn't really blame him. I hadn't made that part clear.

I shook my head. "You wouldn't be paying me. I'll put your name on the list of favorite clients. Not many of us have people we're willing to have sex with for free while we're inside Asiq, and if I have someone booked, I can't move them back so that you can stay longer at that point, but there is a list, and I can put you on it. Then you'd just have to tell the guy at the front podium your name when you came in, and I'd get a message on my com."

Em didn't look happy about even that offer. However, it was the most I could give him. "I don't want you going back there."

"That's not up for negotiation, Em." I stepped toward him, ready to try to placate him with kisses, but he moved back from me.

If that's how he wanted to do things, that was fine with me. One night of sex and I was back to being an aspasian and he was a bounty hunter where not even us being friends was an option. I tried not to feel annoyed with him and his decision. "I have to leave in an hour." I really didn't need to be gone that soon, but I didn't want to hang around in my apartment with him either. "You have until then to be ready before I kick you out, Emmanuel."

Saying his name, letting him know I didn't see him as "Em" anymore, seemed to help shake him out of whatever he'd been so focused on a second before. He frowned at me, gave me a single nod, then went into my shower. I was having some juice in the kitchen when he came out of the bedroom fully dressed and apparently ready to go.

"There should be no one else on your tail now that the senator is dead," he said briskly as he strapped his neutralizer guns back to his hips and buckled the holsters around his thighs. "Because of this, I expect no more payment from you."

"Of course." I didn't move from the counter I was leaning against.

He straightened up and looked right at me. "And I expect no more contact from you either."

It was cruel of him to cut me out of his life so quickly, but I supposed that was to be expected in a way. He said he didn't do intimacy often, that it didn't go with being a bounty hunter. And no matter what his reasons had been, if he'd even had any, I had no intention of no longer being an aspasian anytime soon.

Being mad at him for long, though, was an impossible task, and I wasn't about to let the final words between us be laced with anger. Putting the glass in my hand into the sink, I stepped away from the counter and went to him. "Take care of yourself," I said, coming up so close to him that the tips of our shoes brushed together. "No unnecessary risks. Don't die out there."

He swallowed thickly and gave me one slow nod. "If you change your mind…."

"I won't." Taking a chance, I reached up and ran my hands down his chest. "If you want me, you'll have to take me as an aspasian." He covered my hands with his, keeping me close.

I'd never seen him look so sad, so absolutely miserable as he stared down at me, than he did in that moment. "I can't do that. It is an impossible choice that you're asking for. No man would share someone he cares about with so many others."

I shrugged, refusing to let his words take seed in my heart and give me the doubt I'd been pushing away for so long. "Maybe, maybe not. I figured out a long time ago that this is who I am and what I enjoy doing. If you want anything with me, this is me, and I won't change for you or anyone else."

"Because you like having sex with random people?" He didn't even try to hide the disgust in his voice.

I lifted myself up to the tips of my toes and kissed his shiny, silver cheek. "No. Because I like making people happy." When I stepped back, he released me without a word. "I meant what I said. You'd be welcome in Asiq. And if you showed up here in two weeks, I wouldn't turn you away. But you have to accept me as I am if you want anything at all from me. Even if you just want to be friends."

"I can't do that."

I knew that well enough. Not many people could accept an aspasian in their lives, even if they weren't romantically involved with them. I'd been lucky in that the people I'd known didn't judge me badly for what I did. Some had even gotten off on it. But that was all in the past, and those friendships and brief physical encounters hardly mattered now.

For a moment I wondered if I was asking too much of him and everyone else I'd ever had to defend my choices with to accept that part of my life. But I decided that I really wasn't. What I did and who I was with were my choices. No one forced me to be an aspasian. I loved what I did, and I cared about each and every person I was around while I was there. It may not have been fair of me to say that I wouldn't be giving it up for Emmanuel, or anyone else for that matter, but maybe it wasn't right of him to ask me to either.

"Take care of yourself," I told him. I went back to the kitchen, poured him another glass of juice, and put a travel lid on it. When I came back to him, he'd hardly lifted his head to look at me. I offered him the glass anyway. "For the trip, wherever you're going. If you get thirsty."

That got me a small smile, but it was a far cry from what he'd given me the night before while he'd been in my bed, his body flush against mine, his panting breath hot against my neck. I blushed as I remembered the feeling of him coming in me, the way he whispered my name against my neck afterward.

He took the cup from me, and I headed to the door before he could see how hard I was and think, wrongly, that my body's response had anything to do with me looking forward to going back to Asiq. How I would have loved to be able to pull him back into my bedroom and have him to myself for the next hour.

Emmanuel followed me onto the steel catwalk that ran between the apartments and up to the docks where both of our shuttles waited for us. I watched him get into his first, then shook my head at my stupidity as I suddenly became upset that he hadn't even turned back to say good-bye to me before getting in. I was strapped into my shuttle a few minutes later. In my hurry to get him out of my apartment I'd forgotten the duffel bag I usually took with me to Asiq, but I kept a spare stash of clothes on the shuttle in case I got held up somewhere or got dirty doing something, so I knew I'd be okay for a while. I'd remembered my com, which was the important thing.

I looked through my missed messages once I was away from the space station. My shuttle was set to autopilot, and I didn't worry about it getting me to Asiq as I looked through my spam notes. The only one of any interest to me was a picture of Thierry getting yet another award pinned to his jacket. I couldn't believe he looked as old as he did, and it made me feel impossibly ancient to realize my little brother was closing in on thirty. I shouldn't have been of an age to have a brother quite that age, but he looked good and happy. That was the most important thing. I wrote back *Congrats* to him, then sent the note off.

FOUR HOURS later I was on the landing platform on Wish and heading toward Asiq with the sun shining down on me. I gave a nod to Monroe then went into my room. It was my home away from home, my sanctuary, so I should not have felt as empty as I did while lying down on the bed. I wouldn't give up being an aspasian, but that didn't mean I couldn't have more than that either. Did it? I wasn't so sure. Easy, random sex I could deal with. I got that at home, and I had plenty of that here in Asiq. But what I couldn't get out of my head, was the vulnerability, or the need, that I'd seen in Emmanuel's eyes when he'd been over me. It was more than the way he'd had sex with me. It was more than the why he'd whispered my name as he'd come, like I was somehow precious. I didn't know exactly what it was that made Emmanuel stick in my mind, but I couldn't escape thoughts of him even as I lay under my first client since being back in Asiq. Even the third man to be with me that night couldn't chase away the sight of Emmanuel's face as he'd found his pleasure with me.

I lay there that night wishing I could speak to someone, anyone, about what I was feeling. And, finally, at close to midnight, I realized I could. I got out of bed, put on a shirt, and headed out of my room and down the first hall on my left when I came to the fork. Some of the guys were still working this late. I'd been off for at least an hour. It might have even been two. I hadn't been paying much attention to what time I had finished up with my final client.

I knocked on Monroe's door and was surprised to see that he was still awake as well. I'd expected him to be asleep, but there wasn't a trace of sleep in his expression at all as he stepped back and let me in.

"You were quiet when you came in tonight," he said as he closed the door behind me.

I nodded and sank into one of the comfortable chairs across from his desk. "I had some stuff on my mind."

"Anything with Thierry?"

Smiling, I shook my head. My brother was fine and, from every note I received from him, very much still in love with Monroe. "Whatever you did to get him to fall in love with you, it worked. I wish I knew your secret."

Monroe laughed as he sat down on the other side of his big desk. "I wish I did too. Then I could use it against him when he's mad at me. Your brother can be stubborn."

"Our father was too."

"That must be where you both get it from."

It was good to talk about Thierry with Monroe, since he was such a safe subject between us. But talking about my brother didn't change the fact that I still had a lot on my mind.

"Are you having trouble with love?" Monroe quietly asked me. Once, years ago, we'd been the kind of friends who could talk openly about relationships. We had even been able to joke about who was into who in the club, which Monroe had never cared about as long as it didn't interfere with our work. Since he and Thierry had gotten together, though, it had felt strange to talk about such things with the man who was in love with my brother.

Was I having trouble with love? I repeated his question in my head. It was so simple and yet so complicated because I refused to give up who I was for the sake of someone else's comfort and security. "Do you think there is a man in the universe who would accept someone who stayed an aspasian, despite being with him?" I was thinking about Emmanuel, but I wasn't set on him being that person. He'd shown me plainly that he wasn't willing to be the kind of man I needed, the type I knew I deserved.

Monroe looked at me seriously for a long time, and I let my mind wander to what it might be like to have someone stay with me for more than a few hours, or even a night. To not have to do a comcall with them when I wanted to see them, and not to have sex expected as soon as they arrived. Sometimes that was fine, sometimes it was even nice to be wanted so badly that the door couldn't even close fully behind him before he was taking his pants off and ready to screw me against the kitchen wall. I'd had that more than once, and with more than one lover. I was ready for something more, something that meant more than sex, something where coming over and talking on the couch was considered a date. Where staying over for a weekend and falling asleep together didn't result in me waking up alone without a note to say good-bye.

Maybe what I wanted was love, but I was seriously starting to doubt that love for someone who was determined to stay an aspasian really existed.

"Do you want there to be?" Monroe asked me, interrupting my tumbling thoughts.

I nodded without thinking about his question fully. Yes, I wanted to find someone who could accept all of me.

Monroe put his hands together softly and leaned across the desk, bringing us closer together. "Why not just stop being an aspasian? Retire, go home, love someone. There are plenty of men out there who can get over the life of a former aspasian. Or, if you wanted to lie about that, you could say that you've been working for me in the kitchen for the past twenty years. That's only half a lie."

I could see the uncertainty in his eyes, the doubt. He didn't want to let me go. Maybe it was just about the money I brought in. But I was certain it was more because he thought that somehow he'd lose Thierry if I wasn't around anymore. There was no chance of that. Thierry was too far in love with him to turn back now. If lying to him for months and hiding his identity hadn't turned my little brother off Monroe, nothing would now.

"That's not going to happen. I enjoy it too much. It's so much more than the sexual pleasure I get when I'm with my clients. It's what I'm able to give them. How I can make them smile or laugh. Or how I hold them while they cry and tell them everything is going to be okay, and they look at me like they actually believe me for that second." I smiled just thinking about it. I loved my work, loved what I did. I wasn't a whore, I was an aspasian, and we took care of our clients in a way no one else could. I knew their darkest selves, those secrets they didn't want to tell anyone else, and I accepted them as they were with open arms.

"I'm blessed to have you around," Monroe said. I looked up at him to see him smiling. "And I'm glad you won't be leaving me. But I do hope you can find someone who will take you as you are. You deserve that. And you absolutely deserve to be loved. Since Thierry…." His smile turned even brighter and I could see the love coming off him as he thought about my brother. I'd long since given up any hope of being able to protect Thierry somewhere out there in the universe so now it was simply that I was happy for them both. I wanted to see them stay together forever. "Since I fell in love with Thierry," Monroe began again. "I feel better. Fuller. Like all the little annoying things all of you do constantly isn't so much of a concern."

I snorted as a grin touched my lips. "Some of them aren't so bad."

An eye roll was my only answer, but Monroe was still smiling. He loved his money, but he did like some of us. I wasn't willing to say that he wouldn't have thrown some of us off the planet, though, at one point or another if he could have. "Do you need to take tomorrow off? I can put you in the kitchens for the evening."

"No, that won't be necessary. I'll be fine. Just thinking."

"That's understandable." I saw his attention go to his vidscreen. "Was there anything else?"

I knew when I was being asked to hurry up and leave. "Are you expecting someone?"

I'd never thought I'd see the day when Monroe blushed, but suddenly he was. "A vidchat with Thierry, actually."

And by the looks of it, this was one call I didn't want to be around for. I rose quickly from my chair. "Good night, then. Thank you for taking the time to talk."

Monroe nodded. "Good night. If you change your mind about the kitchens, let me know tomorrow morning before your first client comes in."

"I will." I hurried to the door and the sound of a call coming in followed me out into the hall.

CHAPTER
FIFTEEN

FALLING BACK into my life at work was easy and required almost no thought from me as I went through the motions of what was expected of me while I was at Asiq. I'd been an aspasian for the better part of my life. Dancing with the men I worked with, showing off for clients, serving them in whatever way they wanted… it was all completely normal to me. I should have been happy. I shouldn't have been thinking about Emmanuel nearly as much as I was. He didn't deserve my thoughts, my constant attention.

I lay under my clients as they rocked into me, crying out and gasping against my neck, and I pictured him above me. I thought of his body covering mine, his silvery skin under my fingertips, and the hard nubs that ran along the backs of his arms and up his shoulders brushing against the palms of my hands. And I missed him. As stupid and irrational as that thought was, I did miss him. And a part of me hated him for that, for making me miss him, and want him, as much as I did.

I lay in bed, with a bowl of chocolates beside me on the sheet, as I ate far more than I should have, and thought not just about Emmanuel, but actually what I wanted in a relationship. If I had someone waiting for me back at the station, I wouldn't bring anyone else there. I'd be exclusively theirs unless I was at work. And I would want them to be mine as well, but not only for two weeks. I would want to know, absolutely and without question, that I was the only person they were ever with.

It may have been unfair that I couldn't give them the same certainty, and actually it probably was, but I knew with everything

I was that I would not give up being an aspasian for anyone. No matter how much I cared for them or how much they wanted me. I needed to work, to feel useful, and none of the myriad of jobs I'd done while I'd been struggling to keep Thierry fed those first few years after our parents' deaths paid as well as being an aspasian. And none of them made me feel as good about myself, or the work I did, as this job did.

At the end of the day, I loved who I was and what I did while I was here. I enjoyed spending time with the other guys who worked here, and there were times, when my two weeks were up and Monroe was telling us to go home, that I didn't want to leave. I had fun here, and I didn't want to give that up. I wouldn't.

I also wanted love, though. I wanted someone who would hold me simply because they wanted to, because they enjoyed having me nearby. There had to be someone out there who would whisper his love for me against my neck as he stroked into me, leisurely taking his time as if there was no rush to get off, as if he wasn't being charged by the hour.

Someone like that had to exist out there somewhere. I was naked as I lay there eating chocolates. Not having clothes on didn't bother me in the least. I didn't like them much anyway, never had, and being an aspasian didn't do anything to diminish that side of myself. I spent most of my day with at least pants on, but that didn't mean I had to like it. As I lay there now, though, with the expensive sheets rubbing against my skin, I decided to enjoy the pleasure I hadn't found with any of my clients all day. Not coming with them was strange, but most hadn't noticed. The one who had, a man nearly a decade younger than myself, had needed quite a bit of gentle reassurance while I told him he had nothing to do with my lack of enthusiasm in that regard. I'd kept him on for another hour, at no charge, while I'd pleasured him with my mouth and brought him to another orgasm. My lack of one didn't seem to matter too much to him after that as he'd kissed my cheek through the haze of his pleasure and somehow managed to stumble down the hallway as I walked him out of Asiq.

Now, though, now I could take what I wanted. I could imagine whatever I wanted, picture anyone I wanted with me as I gently cupped my sac. I was already half hard, and if I could find the right images, I knew it wouldn't take me long to find my own pleasure and drift off to sleep. The only image that came to me, though, was one of Emmanuel on his knees between my thighs, his head bent over my cock, his silvery lips tight around my head. My body responded instantly to that idea and, shrugging it off, I went with it, letting myself get wrapped up in the moment as I brought my hand to my base and began stroking myself.

In my fantasy he was gentle with me. He took his time sliding his lips down my shaft and running his tongue up the underside of my head. I roughly stroked myself as I squeezed my cock, wishing it was his mouth and not my hand that warmed my skin. I pulled some lotion over from the nightstand next to me. It was the same bottle I'd used to give Emmanuel a back massage weeks before. Remembering his thick muscles and scarred skin, rough under my fingertips, made me groan as I slicked the white liquid over my cock. I couldn't help thinking about what it looked like and dropped some over my stomach before rubbing it in, wishing it was actually his come and that he'd just released himself over me after riding me hard.

The time for gentleness was over as I stroked my hand over my slicked up cock and played with my balls, bucking off the bed as I thought of Emmanuel being in me, his cock filling me as his hands dug into my hips. My orgasm bolted through me, and I arched my back and closed my eyes as I rode it for as long as I could. Lights danced behind my eyes, and I bit my bottom lip as I shook.

Coming down from my orgasm was nearly painful, and the loss of warmth as I remembered that I was still alone made me shake my head. I felt worn out, defeated, and a bit lost. Thinking about Emmanuel could make me come, hard too, but I wanted him there with me. I deserved to be understood too, and appreciated for what I was and what I could do. And he wasn't able to give me any of that.

I cleaned up quickly and looked back to my bed. I was too energized now for sleeping, so I put on some light pants, and I made my way out to the lounge and fixed myself a drink. A bit of spicy alcohol, some citrus, and I had something tolerable that was decent enough for me but that I wouldn't have served to any client I actually cared about. I didn't mind. I'd experimented. It was good enough for now. I could have made a smoothie, but even looking at the machine reminded me of Emmanuel. And, I told myself, the music played as the guys danced on stage for the clients, and running it would have been distracting.

It was only half a lie, but it worked to get me away from the bar area and over to the lounge. A client pulled me onto his lap, and we both laughed as I fell onto him. His arms tightened around me, holding me close against him, letting me feel his erection through his trousers. I grinned at him over the rim of my glass as I took a sip.

This was me acting in the purest sense of the word. I wasn't interested in taking a client back to my bed. I'd been ready to go to sleep only a little while ago. But coming out to the lounge meant I was available for appointments. That was Monroe's rule, and it made sense. There was no reason for one of us to be out there, flirting and laughing with the clients, if we weren't interested in having some company. And it wasn't fair to the men who came to Asiq to want one of us only to hear that we weren't available for their pleasure.

"Take me back to your room," he huskily said against my neck. His words were a rough caress against my neck, one that wasn't particularly welcome, but I didn't argue. I smiled, put my drink down, and took his hand before sliding off his lap. He grabbed a handful of my butt through the light pants I'd thrown on before coming out of my room, and I turned back to him with a smile. I didn't recognize him, but then again I was usually in bed by this time, so that wasn't all that strange. Maybe he was a regular who only came late at night. I knew some people preferred the mornings. I had one client who I was ready for at seven in the morning sometimes. They were nice enough to give me advance notice of their appointment so I could make sure to be awake and completely functional for them before their arrival.

This man yanked me away from my room by my hand once we were close and pushed me against the wall in the hallway. He kissed me roughly, his calloused hands digging into my stomach as he shoved his tongue into my mouth. I went soft under him, yielding to his touch, his desires. I didn't flare open for him. I was too tired and filled with too much pain to open myself up for him in that way. But I accepted what he wanted to give me without a single sound of complaint.

I was an aspasian. If I couldn't be with someone when I wasn't feeling my best, then I had no right to lay claim to that title. I was an actor, an entertainer, and I used my body to bring my clients pleasure. I was distracted, I couldn't help that, but I could give him as much of me as I was possibly able to. I managed to get us into my room and was barely able to close the door behind myself before he had me up against the wall again, this time with my chest against it. He yanked down my pants, and I relaxed every muscle in my body as I prepared myself for his intrusion.

"If we had time I could have enjoyed this with you more," he groaned against me as he brought me back against him.

As far as things to say when someone was about to have sex with me, it was a bit strange. Feeling something cold against the back of my neck, that was the big surprise, though. I tried to twist around to see what he was doing, but he pressed his palm between my shoulder blades, holding me still. I trembled.

"What are you going to do to me?"

I was too far away from the panic button against the headboard, and I knew, without even being able to look over my shoulder, that he was blocking any view Monroe had of us. If Monroe was watching us at all, which I wasn't sure that he would be since I was supposed to be off the clock by now, he'd only see a guy screwing me against the wall.

He ran his hand that was between my shoulders around my ribs and down my stomach, bringing us closer together. Whether he thought we were being watched, and wanted to put on a show, or if he was taking advantage of my inability to move without possibly hurting myself with whatever was poking me in the back of the neck, I didn't know.

But right then I didn't care.

I spun to the side and brought my fist out, catching him on the side of the face as I came away from the wall. Before he had a chance to react I was kneeling over him, my knee braced in the middle of his chest and keeping him pinned down, while I punched him square in the face. Blood from his broken nose spurted over my floor and splattered across my knuckles. Against my purple skin, it was hardly noticeable, though, and I ignored the sticky feeling of his thick blood as it clung to my skin.

The thing he'd held at the back of my neck had been a neutralizer gun, and without thinking, I shot him in the shoulder. He contracted under me, his wide eyes and open mouth showing me his shock, though he couldn't say a word. I was sure that it hurt him, but I couldn't bring myself to care about whatever pain he might be in.

Shots from a neutralizer never lasted all that long, though, and before I could get off his chest and fix my pants, he was already starting to twitch his fingers. I shot him again for good measure before I lifted myself off him.

I fixed my pants then sat on the edge of the bed so I could watch him and make sure he didn't get the better of me again. Since Monroe hadn't come rushing in yet to save me, I was fairly certain the camera wasn't on. Taking a chance to test that theory, I looked over to the small circle in the corner of the room and had my suspicion validated. The little red light wasn't on. Only a black circle the size of my thumb stood there. I was all alone with this man, and I decided I deserved some answers.

"Here's how this is going to work," I said, realizing I sounded a bit like Emmanuel in that moment. I didn't consider that a bad thing at all. He had a way of making people listen to him and getting them to do what he said. I only needed a fraction of that right then. "I'm going to ask you some questions. If you answer me to my satisfaction on all of my questions, I'll let you go back out to the lounge. You'll get to walk away from Asiq. If you don't, and I have to keep shooting you to get the information I want, then I'll hand you over to my boss. And no one will ever find your body after that."

I didn't know for sure that Monroe killed people, but I figured he probably wouldn't like people threatening me, not only because of the money I made him, but also because of Thierry. Monroe was so head over heels in love with my brother that maybe I could have gotten away with murdering this guy myself.

He was able to twitch his fingers again, so I lifted the gun up from my position four feet from his left shoulder and prepared to shoot him if he told me anything but what I wanted to hear. "What was your plan tonight?" I began.

"To kill you" came him gruff, pain-filled reply.

This again? I rolled my eyes, despite the seriousness of the situation. "You couldn't know I was going to come out to the lounge. How were you going to get back to these rooms?" No one was allowed back without one of us.

"Get one of you to bring me back. Cause a scene, bring you out, grab you, kill you and the others."

That was a horrible plan. "It wouldn't have ever worked." I was certain about that. And yet, the way he'd said it all, as if it would have been so easy for him to kill me and everyone I worked with, had chills racing down my spine. I was glad I'd come out, if he was half crazy enough to try something like that. "Why were you trying to kill me?"

"Saunders."

That name had me frowning instantly. "He's dead," I said without any hesitation. "Emmanuel killed him."

The man on the floor in front of me laughed dryly and was now able to move his legs. I didn't have much time before I'd have to decide if I was discreetly going to let him go, or if my plan was to shoot him again for more information.

"He shot a doppelganger, someone hired to distract him in just such a time as that." His voice was strong now, and I knew my time was up as he lifted up his legs as if he could manage to launch himself to his feet.

I shot him just to be safe. Then, as he lay on the floor writhing in pain, I put my com back on my wrist and connected myself to Emmanuel.

"It's late," he growled at me.

I didn't give a damn what time it was. At the moment I had far bigger problems than his lack of sleep. "A man who tried to kill me tonight said that you killed a doppelganger and not the senator. What should I do with him, Emmanuel?"

I heard his breath catch, and I knew he was listening to me now. It was good to have his full attention, especially when I needed him as much as I did then. "Where are you?"

"Asiq." I thought he would have remembered that I was going there after our argument before. I was actually surprised he didn't know that straight away.

"And are you safe right now?" I heard him moving around and wondered where he'd been, what he'd been doing, and if anyone was there to do it with him.

As jealousy flared its ugly head in my belly, I tried to focus on what he'd asked me. "Sure. I keep shooting him with a neutralizer."

"I'm on my way. I'll be there in an hour. Shoot him if he so much as twitches a muscle. Do not let him regain any kind of mobility before I get there."

I would have rather that he take care of the Senator Saunders problem, but maybe he needed to take care of my latest problem first. Either way, my heart stupidly sped up at the realization that Emmanuel would be back in Asiq soon. Only…. "To get here that fast you'd have to be on Wish already."

He said nothing to that. "I'll see you soon." Emmanuel hung up on me, and I wanted to throw something at him the moment he came through my door. Instead of hanging on to that anger, though, I checked the guy to make sure he didn't need to be shot again for my safety—I wasn't a sadist who got off just on shooting him for no reason after all—and went to call Monroe.

CHAPTER SIXTEEN

WHEN EMMANUEL knocked on my door, Monroe was already there waiting for him. He opened it and closed it without saying a word as I stared at them both from my place on the bed. I hadn't moved, and the neutralizer was still tightly gripped between my palms. I liked having it there. It made me feel like I had at least some control over this mess when I knew I had absolutely none. If the senator was alive, then I was still in danger, and now Emmanuel had no reason to protect me from him.

Seeming to ignore Monroe, Emmanuel stepped over the prone man on the ground and came over to me. He cupped my cheek, pulling my gaze up to meet his as he looked down at me. "Are you all right?"

It felt far too good to have him holding my cheek as he was. The rough pads of his fingertips caressed my skin, and for a few blissfully perfect moments, I completely forgot where we were and the dire situation I'd found myself in. As the rest of the world quietly floated away, I was left with just Emmanuel and the warmth of his fingers against my skin.

The man on the floor interrupted my quiet, stolen seconds as Emmanuel turned to look at him. He didn't release me, though, not until I forced myself to pull back from his touch. I instantly missed it, and though I'd known calling him was the best thing to do since he would know how to fix the situation, I suddenly wished I hadn't. It was far easier not to think about him when he wasn't right there in front of me.

"I'm fine. Take care of him, and go kill Saunders."

Emmanuel turned to give me a sharp look, and I realized bossing him around might not have been the best move on my part given how our relationship had so quickly deteriorated only that morning. I hadn't been able to go even twenty-four hours without needing him to rescue me from someone trying to kill me again. That realization shouldn't have made me smile as widely as it did.

"Please?"

He huffed at me as he crouched down next to the man. "His name is Braken Logy. A colleague, of sorts. He's not in my class. And the price he demands for a kill reflects that."

"Pretentious, arrogant—"

Emmanuel shot him with his own neutralizer and instantly shut him up. I hadn't even realized Braken had been able to move already. I thought Monroe should have mentioned that, but when I looked to where he'd been standing across the room from me, he was gone. Had I been so lost with Emmanuel that I hadn't even noticed him leaving? Apparently. That surprised me even more than knowing the senator was still out to kill me.

"Where is the senator now?" Emmanuel asked Braken.

"You shot him," I was quick to remind Emmanuel. "He can't speak."

Emmanuel shook his head and pressed a small metallic box to the side of Braken's throat. "You think you know everything about getting information out of someone? You have a lot to learn."

The problem was I didn't want to learn. This bloody, violent business was none of mine. I could have left the room. I trusted Emmanuel enough to get the information he needed to keep me safe. But I didn't want to leave him. I wanted to be there with him, to show him I wasn't afraid of what he did and to prove to myself that I was strong enough to take him on.

There was no reason Emmanuel should have to do the things he did alone. Getting information, I assumed, could sometimes be filled with pain. Not the kind that would physically hurt Emmanuel, but I'd seen him at his softest and most vulnerable. And I couldn't imagine that the man I'd seen when we'd been together would be able to walk away from killing someone without feeling something himself. It would leave him deeply scarred, even more so than the marks on his back.

I reached out to him, only having to lean a few inches forward to do so as he'd been sure to place himself between Braken and me. He froze the instant I laid my fingers on his back. Despite the heavy jacket he wore, I knew where the deepest of his cuts lay, and I traced one as I remembered how rough they'd felt under my palms when we'd been together. It seemed as if it had been so long ago that he'd been in my bed, and I'd given myself up to him without even a hint of reservation. But it was less than a day, and the loss of him hurt me more than I was willing to admit.

"He's hiding out on Tebulon," Emmanuel said, getting back to his feet.

I blinked rapidly, not realizing Braken had even said anything. With him moving away from me, and my hand no longer on his back, he didn't notice me cringe away at the sight of the bloody body at the foot of my bed. I quickly pulled my feet up under myself. I wouldn't ask Emmanuel what he'd had to do. That much was obvious by the act of him cleaning off his knife with Braken's pant leg. I wanted to say something, though. I had to. The silence was like a physical pressure bearing down on me, and I needed him to know I wasn't afraid of him. That I'd understood.

That I was thankful for what he'd done in order to get the information he needed once again to keep me safe.

"Emmanuel?" I said, wishing my voice was stronger as I moved toward the center of the bed to kneel.

His knife apparently as clean as he was going to be able to get it, he straightened up and turned to face me. He said nothing, only looked at me as if he expected me to look down at what he'd done. To condemn him in some way. But I didn't have it in me to do that to him. Not right then, and likely not ever. He wasn't some monster. He was a bounty hunter doing his job, what he'd been trained to do. He was no more vile than I was when I brought a man pleasure in this very room.

"Are you okay?" I asked him, making sure there was no trace of pity in my words.

I didn't reach for him, instead expecting him to come to me if he wanted to. He didn't, which wasn't all that much of a surprise to me, but after a few moments, he seemed to change his mind. That was until we both noticed a bit of blood on the cuff of his shirt as it poked out from beneath the arm of his jacket. He turned his hand over, as if wondering why there was blood there, and I saw more on his palm.

Without saying a word to him, I took his hand, even though there was blood on it, and pulled him into the bathroom with me. He stripped his jacket off without having to be told, and I made the water in the sink warm enough that I thought he'd enjoy it. There were plenty of good smelling soaps and lotions in there. Even a scrub to make our hands softer, but he ignored all of the small bottles as he scrubbed at his skin under the warm spray.

With a tsk I shook my head at him. "Wait. Stop. You're going to hurt yourself if you keep rubbing your hands together that hard. Let me help." I grabbed down my favorite soap mixture, something warm that smelled like the trees that lined the streets of Wish, and put enough on my hands that I knew I wouldn't have to go back for more.

Emmanuel seemed completely unsure of what I was trying to do as I ran my hands over his. "See, like this. You'll still get clean. I promise. But you don't need to scrub your hands raw." With smooth strokes I worked my fingers over his hands. I enjoyed this moment, getting to help him and having an excuse to touch him. Everything wasn't all figured out between us, not by a long shot. But it was nice to pretend, just for a little while, that everything was fine and this was normal for us.

Maybe for someone he let love him this would be. I knew I wasn't that person and, though it hurt to realize I could never be anything more than a temporary mark in his history, I knew how to be an adult about it. Sometimes we didn't get what we wanted. That's how life was. And an aspasian didn't get to have someone love them enough to be okay with what they did with other people behind closed doors. That was asking far too much, and I knew I wouldn't be trying to ask anyone for something like that again. One horrible rejection was enough to last me a lifetime.

"Why are you doing this?" he quietly whispered. His voice was filled with pain, and maybe even a little fear. I was good at hearing the feelings behind voices since so many people lied with their words but a tone combined with body language was the ultimate truth.

I wanted to kiss him, to tell him this was fine, everything would be okay. But I didn't think he'd accept a kiss, and I knew it wouldn't all be fine. Not for me at least. I still had someone out there in the universe who wanted to kill me, and I needed Emmanuel to get rid of that threat for me.

"Because I want to," I said, meeting his gaze in the mirror in front of us. "Because I enjoy touching you."

He dipped his head a little at that, dropping his gaze from mine and leaving me standing there completely unsure of myself. "We can't do this. I can't share you with others."

I knew exactly what he meant, and I didn't blame him as I went to the stack of soft towels sitting on a low bench and handed him one for his hands. On second thought I decided to dry his hands myself. "I've never known someone who could."

"I'm sorry."

His hands were dry, and I dropped the towel, but I wouldn't give up touching him until he told me to stop. I couldn't make myself put that much space between us without his refusal of me and everything I was again. It was stupid, and likely even bordered on masochistic, but I wasn't going anywhere.

"You don't have to be sorry for being completely normal," I told him as I slipped my hands into his and simply let my palms rest against his. He didn't pull away. Instead he looked down at me and gave me a sad little smile.

"Has anyone ever said yes to you in that scenario?"

I had to think back, had really to consider, but I'd known the answer before I'd even started to go back down the twisted memory lane that had been my, very brief, relationship history. "No." And that sucked, but it wasn't exactly surprising either. People wanted to know that the only person with the one they cared about was them. Not being told about it wasn't good enough, and I refused to lie about what I did and where I went every two weeks.

He released my hands, and I instantly missed his contact. But a moment later, he made it up to me as he cupped my cheek with his palm. "I wish I could be that kind of person for you."

The honesty in his voice nearly broke me, and I nodded before turning my face to place a gentle kiss in the middle of his palm. "I know. I wish you could too. There's nothing wrong with not being able to, though. I'm not bad for being who I am, and you aren't either for what you feel. I don't judge you for it; I only wish things could be different between us."

He released me, and I tried not to mind that as he stepped back out of the bathroom. "I'm going after the senator again. I'll kill him for sure this time," Emmanuel promised me. The change in topic was probably necessary. Otherwise I might have begun to cry, which was unacceptable with him around.

The dead body didn't really bother me all that much as long as I didn't think too hard about him. Braken had been out to kill me. He deserved what he got. I staunchly refused to listen to the little voice in the back of my head that chose that exact moment to pipe up and remind me that once upon a time, Emmanuel had been trying to kill me too. That was a minor detail I chose not to focus on at that moment.

What did bother me was that once again Emmanuel was going to rush off to go be in danger. He'd have his neutralizer gun drawn, and he'd get into the senator's house and take him out, likely while getting shot at in the process. I could see it all so clearly, and I didn't want that for him at all. I wanted him safe and bored in my bed. Not off on some mission to kill someone before they finally sent someone competent enough to kill me.

"If you didn't go after him, would he eventually stop?" I knew the answer, but I had to ask him anyway.

Emmanuel shook his head. "Men like Senator Saunders don't stop something halfway. He's been killing every person he's ever paid to be with him for months now, and as long as he's alive, he will continue to send people after you. If you're worried about him, you don't need to be. I won't torture him. His death will be quick. It won't be painless, as death never seems to be in my experience, but he won't suffer like this man did." He nudged Braken with the toe of his shiny black boot.

He was completely misunderstanding what I meant, though, and that needed to change before he left my room again. That little confusion wasn't going to be something I stood for. "Saunders isn't the one I'm worried about. I don't want you getting hurt. You have enough scars on you already. Don't come back to me with more." That should have been obvious to him. At least I thought it had been.

His eyes widened a little, and I realized at the last moment what I'd said that he would find surprising. He hadn't planned to see me again. He'd cut me out of his life and told me not to contact him again. And I'd implied that he'd be coming back to see me. "This is one last thing, just to make sure you're safe, then nothing more," he sternly told me with a shake of his head.

I understood what he was saying, that he expected me to be gone from his life, for our time together to be over. And it hurt just as much as it had the last time he'd said it. I stepped back, giving him enough room to leave me without me hindering his progress. Monroe would take care of the body, somehow. That wasn't my concern.

"No stupid risks, Em. I mean it."

I covered my mouth as soon as I realized what I'd called him. I expected him to be mad at me for the slip, but he only gave me a slow smile. It was the kind of smile that made me think he was fighting it and trying to keep it from me, but eventually his smile won out, and he had no choice but to give out and let me see that warm expression. "I promise. No more letting people who want to murder you into your room."

He was teasing me, but there was a bite to his words, letting me know he was serious about the demand. "I'll do my best."

Emmanuel nodded as if my answer had been sufficient for him. I wanted to kiss him before he left my room, but I stayed right where I was. Kissing him, especially after he'd just killed someone, seemed somehow wrong. But, as I thought about it, I realized that kissing him wasn't the wrong part. I wanted that from him, and everything I knew about Emmanuel didn't scare me in the least. It was that I was suddenly very aware of a dead body in my bedroom that made kissing him impossible. I got back on the bed as if not touching the floor a few feet from where Braken lay would make all the difference in the world.

It didn't, and I couldn't help the way my fingers had suddenly gone cold as I moved to the head of the bed, putting even more distance between him and me.

Emmanuel frowned at me and stepped over Braken as if he was of no importance at all to join me next to the bed. "What's wrong?" he asked me. There was no gentleness in his question, only a demand for me to tell him exactly what was bothering me now. As if the body in my bedroom wasn't a big enough clue. I gestured toward Braken where he still lay, his skin pale from the loss of blood, his mouth slightly open as if he'd been screaming. Had he cried out and I'd been too distracted by Emmanuel to even notice? I shook my head, disgusted at myself.

Emmanuel shook his head and stepped back from me. "I'm sorry you were here to witness me work. He would have killed you, though."

I turned to look up at him as I frowned. "I'm not upset that you killed him. Or that you came to my rescue. Again."

"You're not?" I shook my head. "Then why are you acting this way?"

Sighing with frustration, I pulled one of my legs up to my chest and rested my chin on top of my knee. "Because it should bother me more that someone died near me. I wasn't even paying attention to him after you came in and took over. That's madness. Isn't it?"

"I'd call it trust," Emmanuel replied with a soft smile as he brushed his knuckles down the side of my face, stopping at my jaw to rub his thumb along that line.

I didn't follow what he was saying and only stared up blankly at him. "How do you figure that?" He'd lost his mind. What I'd felt had nothing to do with trust at all. It was something like insanity, though.

Emmanuel chuckled and walked away again, stepping back over Braken as he went to the door. He looked like he actually meant to leave this time. "You didn't need to do anything. You figured out that I could handle what had to be done. So you relaxed. In my book that's called trust. You can figure out your own word for it."

I glared at him as he left.

CHAPTER
SEVENTEEN

EMMANUEL WAS back at Asiq a week later, and this time he'd brought Resan with him. I nodded to them both as I got up from the comfortable chair I'd been sitting in while talking to a client in the lounge. I had an appointment in an hour, so I wasn't available to be booked right then, but people could always reserve their spot on my calendar for later that night or the next day. I came back to the client with his mixture of alcohol and Sedran berry juice and put the glass down beside his arm. Another aspasian caught his attention, and I was soon forgotten. I held no jealousy, though, as some of my colleagues did with me. There were plenty of horny men to go around for all of us.

But having that client distracted meant I was able to mix up two more drinks, creamy smoothies this time, and take them over to Emmanuel and Resan as I perched on the arm of the chair beside Emmanuel. "Good evening," I said to them both. I wanted to ask Emmanuel if I was officially safe, but I didn't want to do it while people surrounded us. No one was paying particular attention to us, but I knew how quickly that could change if something especially interesting was said.

"How's work?" Resan asked me, looking curious and completely lacking an ounce of judgment in his expression. He didn't care that I was an aspasian but he also wasn't interested in me either.

"Fine. Thank you. Busy, as always." It was the polite answer. But I didn't want to play niceties with Emmanuel around. He was hardly looking at me, and I wondered if this was a new development or if it was seeing me working that bothered him so much. "Two questions, Emmanuel." That got him looking up at me. "First, what were you doing on Wish last week?"

He frowned at me and stalled for time while taking his first sip of the drink I'd brought him. "What makes you think I was on Wish?"

I didn't like to play mind games with most people and especially not him. Not someone I'd been intimate with outside of work, not someone I cared about as much as I did him. "You were here within an hour when I called you for help. That means you were here, on this planet. Sometimes it takes me an hour just to get clearance to land. So let's cut through the lies and have you just answer my question. Hm?"

Resan surprised me by belting out a laugh while I was sitting there precariously balanced next to Emmanuel's shoulder. "I like him, Em. You should keep him."

"Would if he'd stop being a whore," Emmanuel quietly admitted.

I shook my head at his choice of words and sighed loudly. "Fine. Don't tell me. Gentlemen, have a nice night." I slipped off the arm of the chair and began to head toward the hallway that would take me back to my room, where I'd get ready for my next client and be just the kind of whore Emmanuel was back to calling me.

Only a strong hand clamping down on my wrist stopped me from walking more than two feet away from them. I looked down at my wrist, at the silver fingers holding me tightly, then looked back to Emmanuel. "Yes?" I hoped he realized how annoyed I was at him through my tone. I didn't think he needed any more of a hint than that. He was at least smart enough to figure that much out.

"Come sit back down?"

I rolled my eyes, more at myself than at him as I took up a new position sitting on his lap. If he didn't like me sitting on his lap, then that was his problem. Without a word he circled his arms around me, and I turned to him with the fakest smile I'd ever used around any of my clients. "Hey, baby, come in often? Don't think I've seen you around here before." I spread my fingers out and ran my short nails down the front of his jacket.

He frowned, and I hoped he hated the act just as much as I did. If he wanted a whore, this is what he'd get. If he wanted me, as I was, as an aspasian, he had to respect me enough to call me one.

"I have proof of the task being done. I can show you the video in your room if you want to verify," Emmanuel said.

He'd brought proof this time, which made me instantly relieved. And he seemed reasonably sure of himself that he'd killed the right person as well. But he'd still called me a whore, and as far as I was concerned, he still needed to fix that before I'd let him anywhere near my room. If he wanted to be alone with me, he had to pay the price, and my mind was on so much more than credits. "Oh kinky, baby. What kind of a video?" I rocked my voice a little higher too as I batted my eyelashes up at him.

With a grunt his face twisted up like he was in actual pain. "Fine. I can't stand to hear you sound like that. You're an aspasian. It's been a long week, and I don't like to see you flirting with other people like you were when we walked in."

"Flirting and fucking are part of my job," I reminded him, the fakeness in my voice gone. I moved to get off his lap, but he tightened his hands around my hips, making sure I wasn't about to leave. That wouldn't quite do, though, since I did have a client to get ready for. "You need to let me go. I have an appointment, and I still need to shower first before he comes to me."

He closed his eyes, took a deep breath, and slowly relaxed his arms around me. He still hadn't opened his eyes when I slipped silently off his lap. I knew that expression, though. I could tell how much my life, my choices, hurt him. I leaned forward to kiss his cheek. "Thank you for protecting me. Again."

Emmanuel gave me a silent nod, and I offered a wave to Resan, who tipped his glass toward me. Heading down the hallway and back to my room after that was as easy as miserably putting one foot in front of the other. My client was on time, he was a regular, and everything went fine. But I couldn't focus while I was with him. Not while I kept wishing it was Emmanuel with me, his big hands pinning me down by my wrists to the mattress, his silvery skin against my mouth, his gasps rough and warm in my ear.

Clearing my head of any trace of Emmanuel was impossible, especially when he was so close to me, and I was sure my client noticed my distraction. But he was too polite to call me out on it as he kissed my cheek after he'd recovered and moved away from me. He was dressed five minutes later. In twenty I'd showered and returned to the lounge.

I saw Resan first and sat down in a chair near him. "See anyone you like?" I asked him softly, under the low beat of the music that pumped around us. This late at night, Monroe turned the music down to let those of us who had earlier appointments sleep undisturbed. The music was still loud enough to be interesting, and we could all find any reason to dance to whatever Monroe put on. Three men took turns dancing together and kissing on the dais in the center of all the lounge chairs. Resan's focus had been on them, but now that I was back in the room, I saw his attention go to them less and less.

"Could be," he answered me with a shrug of his big shoulders as if there was nothing more to say, as if we were talking about pieces of fruit instead of the people I spent two weeks of my life with every month.

I decided to drop it. "Where's Emmanuel? Did he leave?"

Resan looked from me back to the men dancing together in front of us. "He took someone into the hallway." My stomach instantly dropped, and I pressed my lips together to keep from screaming. He did *what*? No. Resan couldn't have been right. Emmanuel didn't tolerate what we did. He'd have no interest in being with any of them. He thought we were whores. He... I took a deep breath and regained control of myself, a fraction at a time, until I felt whole enough to keep myself together without breaking apart at the first harsh word. Emmanuel was just a man, as flawed as any other. I thought he was beautiful in his flaws, but that didn't make me immune to my quickly breaking heart or the jealousy I felt welling up inside me.

"He's trying to figure out what you do here all day," Resan added, completely unnecessarily.

I nodded. We did plenty. A lot of it without our clothes on.

"He's trying to see if he can handle it."

Well that got my attention. "Handle what? Exactly?"

"What you do."

I turned to see Emmanuel looming over me. I hadn't heard him come up. Hadn't seen him come out of the hallway with anyone. "Was he any good?" I asked him bitterly, welcoming and clinging to the bite in my words as I looked up at him.

Thankfully Emmanuel didn't even try to pretend not to understand what I was talking about. "I didn't screw him. I wouldn't. Get up for a second."

"Why?"

With a sigh, sounding very much like he was fed up with me at that moment, just as much as I was with him, he put his hands under my arms and lifted me himself. I didn't even have a chance to right myself back on my feet before he was sitting down and pulling me onto the chair on top of his lap again. I did not want to get comfortable. I could not give into just how damn warm he was. I would not.... Fuck it.

I relaxed against him, and slowly I felt him soften with me as well. As if he'd been waiting for some unknown, completely silent signal from me to know that everything was fine between us. And, I supposed, that it was. I wasn't willing to stop being an aspasian for him, which left me in no position to have anything to say to him when he decided to go off and have sex with my coworkers.

He ran his hand down my bare back then bushed his fingers through the ends of my hair. It was back in a ponytail and fell down to the middle of my back. I liked having him touch me. Having his hands on me was comforting, and I wished I could have this all the time. Maybe without the music or the half-naked guys dancing around us, but simply sitting on his lap like this somehow released this tight ball I hadn't even known had been settling in my gut. I felt content while sitting there with him and having him stroke his fingers down my back.

"Do you still want to know what I was doing here on Wish?" he quietly asked me.

I nodded and watched Resan get up to go dance with one of the guys. "Were you having sex?"

"No. I was looking for work."

I frowned at a point on his collarbone. "On a pleasure planet?" That made very little sense to me. It was… I shook my head. There weren't contracts to be found on Wish. I was certain of that.

He chuckled, and I felt the noise rumble through his clothing and into my chest. "Yes. Plenty of jealous lovers and jilted exes that want to extract a bit of revenge here too. And credits are credits. Unless someone is innocent, I'm not about to turn away a job."

I shifted my position on his lap so I could face him fully, and I laid my hands on his shoulders. Being in Asiq as long as I had, I'd developed a pretty good center of balance, and keeping my weight off his thighs as I got comfortable on his lap wasn't a big deal to me. Back on my home station, all of that experience went out the window, but here I was different because I was an aspasian.

He looked uncertain as he watched me. I cocked an eyebrow at him and gave him a little smile. "Thanks for letting me know."

"You thought I was here to find something else."

There was no accusation in his voice, only quiet observation. And I had nothing to hide. "Yes. I thought you'd been at another brothel. Getting company."

"I wouldn't," he quickly denied.

I walked my fingers from his shoulders, up the sides of his neck, to go to the top of his spine. Running my fingers over the thin skin there, I saw him close his eyes, the briefest hints that he'd found pleasure in my touch, before he was back to looking at me. His gaze searched mine, and I realized, with a flurry of new energy, that he was still trying to figure me out. I liked being a bit of a mystery to him. It left me feeling sexy, even more than I already did with a beautiful man holding me on his lap.

"I'm starting to think you wouldn't. Resan said you were in the hall with someone because you wanted information. Ask me what you'd like to know. I'll be your exclusive source for all things aspasian." I was teasing him with my voice but completely serious in my words. Before he could answer me, though, I leaned forward and gave him a sharp nip on his bottom lip. I must have startled him, because he tightened his hands on my hips, squeezing me through my thin black pants.

"Do you have clients you don't have sex with?" Emmanuel asked.

I blinked at him, wondering what he was getting at, and trying to get ahead of him, because we had talked about this before, and I had thought that he had understood what I'd tried to explain to him then. "Yes. A few." Whatever his endgame was, I couldn't guess what he'd be getting at. I was so used to the games, to playing people and giving them exactly what they wanted, that simply trusting him and letting him ask his questions felt completely new. And yet… I wasn't afraid of what he'd ask. If I couldn't answer something, I'd let him know. Otherwise, I was open to him. The thought should have terrified me. But I was too settled, too comfortable with him, to do much more than whatever he wanted me to.

He nodded as if that was vital information coming from me, instead of the common knowledge I thought it was. I was good for more than sex, after all. "Do they pay you less?"

"I take less from them," I clarified for him. He lifted his hand from my right hip and gestured as if he wanted me to continue with my explanation. "I've known many of them for a long time. Most of my clients are regulars. I'm usually too booked up with them to take on new clients. If I enjoy my time with them, regardless of what we're doing together, I'll often drop my rates. I can't up my prices if a guy is a bit rougher with me than I'd like, but I do believe in rewarding clients I like."

Emmanuel rubbed his thumbs over my hips before moving his hands to cup my butt. He could have simply been making sure I didn't fall backward off his lap. I knew him better than that, though. I wouldn't stop him or even acknowledge what he was doing if he didn't want to be more overt. If he wanted to have a conversation where he kept his hands on my butt, then that's what we'd do. I was too damn happy to have him close to me again to do anything that could result in him changing his mind about him being here with me.

"These clients that get rough with you, what does Monroe do about them?"

"Throws them out," I told him instantly.

Emmanuel didn't look convinced. "He's much smaller than I am, though he is still larger than you. And he's at least a decade older than me. If I'd gone through with my original plan to kill you, there would have been no chance of him saving you."

"Thanks for your vote of confidence in me. You know, I did defend myself against Braken." I rolled my eyes, not at all impressed with his assessment of Monroe's ability to protect us.

Emmanuel shook his head and squeezed my butt. I didn't know if he'd even meant to tighten his hands over my skin. He certainly didn't give anything away to me that would let me think otherwise. "Braken was an idiot, and an amateur. A child could have knocked him out as you did."

I didn't try to keep myself from glaring at him.

Emmanuel took a deep breath then released it before saying anything more to me. It shook through his chest, and I smelled Monroe's chocolates drifting on his warm breath. The action made him seem like he needed time to think, to figure something out for himself. I would have liked to have been in on whatever he was deciding. Especially since I was pretty sure it had to do something with me. "Would you take only clients that you didn't have sex with?"

I knew I'd see the pain there, the hurt reflecting back at me in his eyes the moment I spoke. And I felt truly like a bastard, as I knew the brief glimmer of hope resting there now would quickly be eliminated. And all I had to do was tell him the truth. "No. I wouldn't be an aspasian, then. I'd be a therapist, and I want to be more than that. I like being more than that. I need to be. And what would you offer me, if I could give you that?"

"Me…," he softly told me as he met my gaze. "You'd have me."

125

I bit my lip and slowly shook my head. "Emmanuel…."

"Em. You can call me Em. Always."

Nodding, I leaned forward and rested my forehead against his as I closed my eyes. "Em. I can't change who I am or what I want. I'm sorry, but I won't. I want you, but I want this too."

"I can't be with someone who cheats on me," he whispered softly against my lips.

"I know." I shuddered and realized a second later that tears were leaking down my cheeks. I didn't want to move my hands and let go of him, so I let them fall. "Someone out there will love you for yourself and everything you are. And you'll love them, and you'll never once have to wonder about who they're with or what they're doing."

"I already love someone. A fierce little Sythe aspasian who is too stubborn to come away from all of this and be mine." The confession broke on his voice, and I shut my eyes tightly against his words.

But I couldn't stop the truth from coming out of me as well. "And I love a bounty hunter who I worry about every minute he's not with me."

He moved his hands from my butt to my back, circling his arms around me and pulling me closer against his chest. I laid my head on his shoulder and shook as my nearly silent cries rocked through me. Em held me for as long as I needed, simply letting me lie there against him. He was gentle and kind with me. And I felt my resolve slipping away.

"How long are you staying on Wish?" I asked him without lifting my head from his shoulder.

"Tomorrow morning Resan and I will be going to take care of a few contracts."

"It's safer when you go together. Keep doing that, please." I still didn't move, refusing to let go of him.

He kissed the side of my head. "Hunting is always easier, and better, with someone you trust. Will you think about what I've said? About taking only clients that don't want sex from you?"

I didn't know how much of a difference thinking about it would bring. I was stubborn, and there was no reason for me to change

126

anything about myself. Except… if I wanted Emmanuel, that was his bargain. "I will," I promised him. I didn't want to lose him, but I was afraid of losing myself as well. I wasn't some cheap whore who slept with whoever came to me for a bit of credits. I was style and grace. I gave the people who paid for my time an experience. I'd been an aspasian for so long I didn't know how to be anything else. It was so ingrained into who I was that I was afraid to let it go and see who that left me as.

We stayed like that for the next hour, until I took Emmanuel's hand and took him back to my room where we lay together for the rest of the night until Resan came to get him the next morning.

CHAPTER EIGHTEEN

MONROE WAS as easy to find as ever two days later, when I'd thought over everything I needed and wanted. They were completely different concepts. I needed my job. I wanted to be an aspasian. I needed to eat, but I wanted the kind of food, the luxuries, Monroe gave us while we were in Asiq. Emmanuel, he fit somewhere in the middle. I wasn't ready to say that I needed him. Not yet. But I could feel how perilously close to that edge I truly was. I also wasn't entirely sure I wasn't ready to throw my arms back and jump without a second thought if only Emmanuel looked at me as he had when we'd been together back in my bedroom on the station.

I knocked on Monroe's door and waited for him to let me in. He was on a comcall, but he came to the door anyway and stepped aside so I could join him in his office. His usually tidy desk was in a bit of disarray, and without thinking, I went to straighten the stacks of papers I saw there. Most people used holoscreens. Monroe was a throwback with his paper. It was expensive and archaic, but it was one of the things he preferred, and the rest of us didn't question. Once his desk was as tidy as I was going to be able to make it, I stepped back and waited for him to get off the call so we could speak.

I had my wish a minute later as he pulled the earbud away from his ear and rubbed at the inside of his ear. "These things seem to get more painful each time I use them. Sit down, Corbin. Is there something you needed?"

I took a breath and stretched my hands out in front of me on his desk as I got comfortable in the chair. "I'm trying to find a compromise with Emmanuel. I won't stop being an aspasian, but he's asked me to think about only taking nonsexual clients."

Monroe nodded and leaned toward me as well. "And? What have you thought about it?"

I wasn't entirely sure, even as I sat there across from him. "I don't believe I have enough clients like that to warrant keeping me here. They also pay less...." I shook my head. I couldn't be both an aspasian and Emmanuel's partner. There was just no way. It was a stupid, foolish dream anyway. And I should have learned long ago, back when I was working in the mines and getting sick every night, that being a fool would never get me anywhere. It didn't pay the bills, it never put food in my belly, and it certainly hadn't kept me safe for those long days spent in the mines.

"That's true. They do pay less."

I nodded.

"But... if having Emmanuel is that important to you that you're willing to compromise on something you love, then let's figure out a way that things might be made to work."

I looked up at him as hope unbelievably flared to life in my heart.

"Someday soon I have hope that Thierry will come back to me. I will be here when he does. But after that I plan to take him far away from here, to a bedroom where only I have the key and where I can have him all to myself and not have to share him with an entire universe. I plan to keep him there until we are both old and gray."

I snickered and knew better than to mention he was already getting a bit gray around the edges of his short hair. That would earn me no favors where Monroe was concerned. "If you want my permission to kidnap my little brother, you don't need it. You have my blessing. Go make each other deliriously happy."

Monroe laughed and shook his head. "Thank you for that. But, no. What I meant was that, at some point in the future, I want you to take over as manager of Asiq. I'll still be the owner, but I want you to handle the day-to-day activities and requirements here. And you would have your own permanent room here too."

I only stared at him, unblinking in my shock. "You want me... to run this?" I waved my hands above my head. I didn't even have words for how big of a responsibility Asiq was, or how very ill equipped I was to handle running a brothel.

"It isn't like it's hard. Listening to you all come to me with your whining problems is the most difficult part of my day. And I do include you in that number, just so you're aware."

"I'd never presume to be exempt," I said with a smile. The teasing I could handle. That was a safe place for us. "But.... Monroe...." I couldn't even begin.

"I was going to ask you anyway as soon as Thierry was back. And I won't be giving you the reins permanently. You'd still be answerable to me in everything that had to do with Asiq, and if my beauty goes up in flames under your watch, I will have your head."

"I know nothing about running a brothel," I reminded him, as if he couldn't already know that for himself.

Monroe snorted and crossed his arms over his chest as he stared me down. "You've been an aspasian in my employ for twenty years. You may not know the minor business details, but you'd learn those quickly. Everything else you already know, already have inside you. I don't doubt you'd do just fine in this role. And I would train you well. We'd go slow, and I would make sure you had everything you needed, all of your questions answered, before I left with Thierry on that oh so magical day that he returns to me. If he ever does."

"I don't question his intent in that regard." I was already thinking past Thierry, though, to the idea of running my own brothel when Monroe was away. But I came back to the same problem as before. "I don't want to give up those clients who need me. I'll stop having sex with the others, but the ones who need someone to talk to, someone to cry with, someone to simply hold them while they sleep for an hour, I won't abandon them."

"I understand. If your intent really is to give up the sexual side of being an aspasian, then I would make you my assistant as soon as you were ready to take on the added responsibilities. You'd need a month to phase out your clients who you are intimate with now and find them new aspasians, but I wouldn't give you new clients that were interested in sex in that time. And as my assistant, just as my manager, I would want you living here so that you can handle things as they come up and not have them be pushed back two weeks to when you could deal with them again. Could you leave your space station?"

My answer was instant. "In a heartbeat." It had been my home for years but I only truly felt relaxed when I was at Asiq. The station was merely a place for my things, and ever since Thierry had moved on, it had seemed more like four steel walls and a few pieces of furniture than an actual home.

"Think it over. I don't want your answer now. Give yourself a few days to decide then come back to me."

I had my answer ready for him, but I understood him wanting me to wait, to give it some real consideration. I only hoped that the compromise was enough for Emmanuel to want to be with me still.

CHAPTER
NINETEEN

I SAW Emmanuel later that week, this time without Resan. I did hear his voice through a doorway before the door was shut, however, so Emmanuel wasn't alone. I was glad they were going out together. Emmanuel was in far too dangerous of a line of work to be going it alone. I smiled at him as I came into the lounge, intent on getting some more chocolates. I had a shirt on with my pants, which was unusual for me. But I wasn't working that morning so I didn't feel the need to grab attention to myself as I usually did.

"Hello," I said, getting comfortable on the seat next to him and offering him one of the chocolates in my hand before they began to melt. He took one and unwrapped the delicate paper around it.

"You look…." He scanned me, and I thought it was a bit insulting that he had to take a few seconds to figure out a suitable compliment for me. "Rested."

I chuckled and laid my head comfortably on his shoulder. The act was one of familiarity, one I didn't know if he'd accept from me. But he brought his hand around my side anyway and rested his fingers on my hip, keeping me close beside him. "I am rested."

"Business is slow, then?"

There was hope in his voice. As comfortable as we were, I didn't want to talk to him about my new choices out in the open of the lounge. "Come back to my room with me?" I tried to keep the heat out of my words, but I knew I failed when he blushed.

"I can't…." He shook his head, looking confused by his own reaction.

Turning my face up to his, I kissed him on his cheek. "Just to talk. If you want more after, then you know I won't say no to you."

"Because you're an aspasian and you have to have sex with whoever wants you while you're here?"

Smirking, I lifted myself off the couch and out of his hold. "No, darling. Because I want you just as much as you've ever wanted me. And, yes, I am an aspasian. But that doesn't mean I get on my knees for just anyone. Now, want to go talk?"

Without a word he got up as well and followed me back to my bedroom. Talking apparently wasn't what he wanted, though, because as soon as the door closed behind us, his hands were on my butt, and he had me pulled tightly against him. I didn't mind the change in plans at all and eagerly lifted my mouth to his for a kiss.

He pushed me against the wall, holding me there and grinding against me, letting me know he was just as desperate for me as I was for him. I groaned against his mouth, needing to taste him, loving the sweetness of the chocolate on his tongue. Before I'd had a real chance to savor him, though, he had me spun around so that my face pressed to the wall. I was in the same position and nearly the same place as Braken had put me, but I didn't think about that as Emmanuel put his thumbs into the band of my pants and yanked them down to my thighs.

"You're stunning," he growled against the back of my neck, making me blush. I smiled when I heard a zipper, and when I felt cool gel slide between my cheeks, I knew he was going to take the time to prepare me for him.

I arched back toward him, letting him know I wanted him too. He slid a slick finger into me, then another, and slowly stroked me as if I was some delicate thing that couldn't handle him. I shook my head before looking back at him over my shoulder. "Em?"

"Yes?" His voice was rough with need, just as I was sure mine was.

"Faster. I won't break."

"Last time—"

I nodded. Last time wasn't perfect. "It'll be okay. Trust me not to let you hurt me? To tell you if you're too rough or don't take enough time with me. Please?" I was barely able to speak as I stood there needing him and yet being denied by him at the same time. It was completely unfair.

He stilled his fingers inside me. "Do you trust me to stop then if you did tell me it was too much?"

"Yes." I knew that instantly. If I told him I couldn't take it, he wouldn't push me. He was never cruel, never mean. If anything he was far too worried about hurting me when he didn't need to think about things like that. I wasn't some doll ready to break at the slightest harsh word or wild bit of sex. I trusted him to stop just as much as I trusted him not to need to be told to.

He slid his fingers out of me, and I watched him over my shoulder, catching his gaze and holding it when he put one hand on my hip and I felt the blunt tip of his cock pressing against my hole. "I didn't come here for this," he whispered, even as he pushed past my ring and gave me his first few inches.

I didn't think he had, but I understood need, and we'd both been denying ourselves. I wanted this too, and I was hard enough that I was sure I'd come against the wall after only a few strokes. Especially when he thrust hard into me, sheathing himself within me and making me gasp as I rubbed my cheek against the wall.

Before I'd even had a chance to recover from the sheer bliss of having him back inside me, Emmanuel had already wrapped his hand around my cock. He didn't squeeze, didn't stroke me, only gave me a tight hold that I found myself sliding into each time he thrust.

"I don't want you to move," he told me, sounding uncertain, even of himself. His voice was ragged, and his thrusts were wild, telling me just how much he needed me, how out of control he really was in that moment.

"I'll do whatever you say." He looked up and met my gaze. My words weren't a game or a tease as they would have been with a client. I was promising him that I was his, and that he could do whatever he wanted with me.

He tightened the hand on my hip and plowed into me harder and faster than he had been before. I kept my gaze locked with his, wanting to know the exact moment he found his pleasure. I wanted to sear that moment into my brain, to take his expression and hold it within myself where no one could ever take it away from me.

I was so focused on him that I was completely blindsided when my own climax came with a force that left me gasping for breath and unable to keep my feet under me. He held me up as my vision blurred into little more than gray dots, until I finally closed my eyes and stopped trying so hard to make sense of the blurry room.

I felt him stiffen against me, and I forced my eyes open, commanding myself to focus on him so that I didn't miss a thing. He was beautiful, absolutely so, as sweat made his silver skin shine and sparkle. Emmanuel leaned forward, pressing his lips to my cheek, and groaned out his pleasure. I never looked away.

"Thank you," I whispered, the words escaping me before I'd had a chance to pull them back. I didn't thank the people I was with, not like that. Not like I'd meant it as much as I just had with Em. He nodded but didn't lift his forehead from my shoulder where he'd dropped it to rest for a while.

I was in no rush. He could take all the time he needed. The only reason I was still standing was because he was holding me up. If he needed to lean on me for his own support, then I was more than willing to let him.

He slowly slid his softening shaft out of me and fixed my pants before adjusting his own clothes. I wobbled as I moved past him and made my way to the bed where I flopped down with none of my usual grace. Em lay down next to me, and I closed my eyes. I couldn't sleep, since we did need to talk, but simply lying next to him as we both rode through our afterglow was perfect.

I felt him take my hand, and I opened my eyes to give him a soft smile. "How much of a compromise do you need to feel comfortable with me here?" I asked him, deciding now was as good a time as any to begin.

He pursed his lips and turned over onto his back, looking away from me. But he didn't let go of my hand. "I don't want you here at all."

My heart sank, and I was ready to pull my hand back from him, but he tightened his fingers around mine, stopping my retreat. "Do you have a counteroffer?" he asked.

"What if I lived here and worked with Monroe to help keep this place going and took nonsexual clients?" It was the best I could do, and if he didn't accept that compromise, then I didn't know what I would do.

He turned his head to the side to look at me. "I don't know if I'd be comfortable with that. I trust you to tell me when something I do is too much for you. But what if you're with a client who wants to have sex with you, even though they said they didn't, and you're then forced to cheat on me?"

I rolled over onto my stomach and came closer to him, pressing my hip against his. "First of all, no one forces me to do anything. If a client gets weird or mean or if I'm just not comfortable with them for whatever reason, there's a button on the headboard. Also, Monroe watches each time we're with a client to make sure we're okay. There's a little camera in a corner of the wall."

"And once again your safety here comes down whether or not you can defend yourself, and if a man that I could easily incapacitate is able to assist you." Emmanuel shook his head, his face twisted into something surprisingly close to disgust. "You need a bodyguard. You all do. Anything less than that won't suffice. Your personal safety is in jeopardy here."

I ran my fingertips down his arm, ending right at his wrist. "What if I asked Monroe to give you a job here protecting all of us poor, defenseless aspasians?" My tone was teasing but my words couldn't have been more serious. "I worry about you too out there."

"I would have to finish out the few contracts I have…," he said thoughtfully.

Nodding, I leaned down to kiss the inside of his forearm. "And I have another three weeks of my regular clients to phase out completely. Some were easy to hand off to other aspasians, but others I've had for years, and they're going to need a little more time to say good-bye to me."

He swallowed thickly, and I watched his Adam's apple bob as he seemed to get lost in his thoughts. "Three more weeks of knowing you're here, having sex with other people? What about when you go home? Back to the station?"

I placed another gentle kiss on his forearm, this time higher up, in the crook of his elbow. "I took care of my things last week. I live here full time. Not in this room, though. This is my working room. I've got an office and everything now. It has a desk that I'm fairly certain would be sturdy enough for us. If you were ever interested."

"I'm always interested."

His words made me smile, and I laid my cheek over his chest, right on his heart, though the rough material of his jacket didn't really leave my cheek feeling wonderful. But I wasn't about to move.

Emmanuel stroked his fingers down my spine and finished his hand's journey in my hair. "Three more weeks of knowing you're not mine...." I heard the pain in his voice, the hurt, and I frowned.

"I've been yours for months. Having sex with them...." I lifted my head to be able to look at him again. "It's not the same thing. You have my heart. They have my ear for an hour or two. My body if they want it and I agree. They don't touch what we have. They don't even come close."

He didn't look convinced.

"I'll phase them out faster," I offered. There really wasn't much more I could do. "Would you like me to talk to Monroe about giving you a job here?"

"Yes. And, whenever I'm here, I'll be watching the monitors you're on to make sure those clients don't try anything with you."

I smiled at him. "I think I'll like knowing you're watching over me."

"Good. I want you protected and kept safe."

I didn't argue with him that I was a man in my forties who could protect myself when I needed to. The point between us was moot, and he had proven me wrong more than once. Having him around would probably keep me safe, assuming someone else wanted me dead. Even if I never had another contract hanging over my head again or a possessive client wanting to keep me all to himself, I would be happy to have Emmanuel around. He made me feel protected and safe just by being in the same room as me.

It was a weird thing to realize, once I had, that someone could make me feel so secure. I'd been on my own, taking care of Thierry, for so much of my life that relying on someone else had never even come up. And part of me absolutely balked at that idea. I'd taken care of myself just fine. But Emmanuel didn't want to take care of me. He didn't want to coddle me and keep me locked away in some tower like I was pretty sure Monroe thought he'd be able to get away with when it came to Thierry. No. Emmanuel simply wanted to keep me safe. And it was the same thing I wanted to do for him as well. If I could convince Monroe that he would be useful there with us, that we all needed him there, then I could be sure of Emmanuel's well-being. He may get in a fight sometimes, but he wouldn't be shot at, and there would never be another scar on him. I'd make sure of that.

I lifted myself up on my elbows to be able to bend my head and kiss one of his perfect silver nipples. His breath caught, and he sucked in his stomach as I took that pointed nub between my teeth. I wanted to play, to love on him as much as could, but I felt myself already beginning to respond to him as well. Glancing down his stomach as I took his nipple into my mouth and flicked my tongue over it, I could see him begin to stiffen as well.

"Corbin?"

Smiling, I lifted my head to see him watching me intently. "Sh. Let me have my fun with you."

Emmanuel gave me a tentative smile and laid his hand on my shoulder, giving me all the permission I needed to enjoy him as I wanted to.

CHAPTER
TWENTY

HOURS LATER, with Emmanuel napping in my bed, I made my way to Monroe's office. His door was open, so I walked in and met his gaze over his desk. "Do you need to close the door behind you?" he asked me.

I shook my head and took a seat. "Not today. I have a request."

He snorted and moved his holoscreen aside. "Of course you do. You and your brother, always with your requests. Though, I wouldn't mind taking a few from him right now. You on the other hand—" He tsked and shook his head. "—haven't I given you enough liberties yet? I'm already losing my most responsive Sythe aspasian."

"I'm your only Sythe aspasian, Old Man," I reminded him teasingly, before I remembered that I was there to ask him for yet another favor. After taking a deep breath to collect my thoughts, I began. "With all the attacks, granted they were all on me, I believe Asiq needs increased security. And I would like to ask that—"

"Only if Resan joins him," Monroe said, cutting me off.

I cocked my head. "Huh?"

Monroe arched his eyebrows at me. "You were going to ask if I'd consider Emmanuel for a position protecting you all. Weren't you?" I slowly nodded. "Get him to convince Resan of the same need, and I'll take them. But only as a package deal. It won't do me much good to have someone in a position to protect my aspasians if he's constantly in your bed."

"We wouldn't... I mean, not during working hours. And—"

Monroe brushed aside my tumbling words with a wave of his hand. "Though, Resan isn't much better. He was insatiable last time he was here. But his credits are as real as anyone else's. Talk to Emmanuel. Get him to convince Resan to join him here. Trial period of two months. If they don't screw up in that time, I'll hire them on permanently. And they can't take jobs while working here. They're either bounty hunters or protectors and my second line of defense after the automatic screenings. They can't be both."

"Of course."

Monroe nodded to me, the matter apparently settled for him. "And, you have a client in an hour. I see that Emmanuel is still asleep in your room. Should I put you up in a different room?"

"That won't be necessary." He'd been more than good to me since I met Emmanuel. I knew how to work and what my job was. "Sexual client?"

"Yes. Will that be a problem?"

"No. Definitely not." I was quite certain of that as I rose from my chair. Emmanuel knew I needed some time to let the clients he didn't approve of go. He wouldn't be happy about it, but I knew he wouldn't say anything either. At least, I was pretty sure that he wouldn't. I supposed that it was time to test that theory out.

"Good. See that it isn't," Monroe said, dismissing me.

I hurried out of his office. I had plenty to do and not much time to get it done in since I also needed to talk to Emmanuel and make sure he wouldn't blow up in the middle of the lounge while he waited for me to get done with my client. If he'd even want to be in the same building while I was having sex with someone else. I shook my head, not knowing how he'd handle what I was about to say to him.

Emmanuel was awake and dressed when I came back into my room. He smiled up at me from where he was putting on his shoes at the corner of the bed, and I went over to him and gave him a kiss on his forehead. He pulled me down onto his lap and kissed me fully, but as much as I wanted to indulge in the delicious feeling of his mouth running over mine, I didn't have that kind of time. "I have good news and bad news. First off, Monroe says you can stay here and protect all of us. But Resan has to join you, and it'll be a trial period at first."

Emmanuel scrunched up his face as if he didn't love the idea of having Resan around him full time. Or maybe it was the trial period. Maybe he thought Monroe not falling at his feet to accept him as the best bounty hunter turned bodyguard ever was somehow insulting to him. I didn't have time to figure that part out. "Is that the bad news, then?"

"Actually… no." I rubbed my arms as I tried to figure out a way to say this quickly, but also not be a complete jackass about what I was about to be doing in the same bed that he was currently sitting on. "You see, I've got a client coming in less than an hour. And I'll be having sex with him."

I waited for him to blow up on me, for him to demand I call the appointment off or refuse to see the client at all. For a second there I thought he might have thrown me over his shoulder and kidnapped me from Asiq so that we'd never have to have this conversation again.

But he only took a deep breath as he stared at me. "I guess we had to come to this point sooner or later. I'll go out for a while, walk around Wish, maybe get some fruits I can't find anywhere else. And I'll try not to think about someone else being with you, with you kissing them and getting on your knees for them…." He shook his head so hard I thought he might snap his own neck. "No. I need to stop thinking about that. Will you shower after you're done with him and call me to let me know I should come back? I don't want to smell someone else on your skin when I'm kissing you."

"Thank you for not being angry. I know it isn't easy for you. And yes, I'll shower, and I'll call you as soon as I've got this room switched over and I'm ready for you to come back."

He ran his hand over my arm that was around his chest. "Okay. It's only for a few more weeks. And honesty is the most important thing right now. Tell me I matter more to you than him. Please?"

I didn't know why he'd need that kind of reassurance. There was no reason he would, but I went along with it anyway to make sure he had as much as I could possibly give him before I had to leave him. "Yes. Absolutely. I love you, Em. I enjoy my time with my clients, but not like you're probably thinking I do. I don't love them. I don't get hard thinking about them. I don't stroke myself until I come while thinking about anyone but you."

He gave me a soft kiss on my forehead. "I love you too. I believe you when you say you don't love any of them, but I know you must find some physical pleasure from being with them, and I need to find a way to get past that in order to keep my own sanity."

He was right; he did need to figure that out. But I could help him get through it by not rubbing his nose in the fact that I had sex with other people. That I'd been having sex with other people even after having sex with him. He didn't need to know how many or what their names were, but there was no good way to make everything all better between us when what I did wasn't wrong in any way except how it made him feel.

"I need to get ready," I softly reminded him.

Emmanuel nodded. "I know you do. Tell me what the process is, please?"

I decided to be as blunt and as analytical as I could possibly be with him. Maybe it would show him that this wasn't some romantic date I was getting ready for, but that there was a man coming to see me who was simply a client, and I had a job to do.

"Changing the sheets and blankets, showering, making sure I'm clean all over, putting on new pants, wiping down the bathroom in case he wants to use it to shower when we're done, then putting out fresh chocolates. If he's in the lounge and a regular, I may go out there, make him a drink, and sit with him for a few minutes before his session begins. But generally they come to the door, I open it, and we begin."

"Then after they leave?" Emmanuel asked me, wisely not bothering with the details between the two points.

I kissed his cheek. "Same thing. I change the bedding, shower again, get on new clothes. We go through a ton of laundry here. If I need some time to relax, I may take a nap, read a bit on my holoscreen, or just sit on my butt for a while. If I'm awake and ready to hang out with other people again, I'll head down to the lounge. Get something cold to drink since it's always summer here on Wish, maybe dance a bit with the other guys, or just hang out and talk to clients. I don't need to throw myself at the clients like some of the guys do. I haven't had to since my first few months here when I started getting regulars. Are you okay?"

Emmanuel slowly nodded. "Yes. Thank you for explaining all that. I think...." He sighed and ran one of his hands over his head. "It won't be easy, but I believe I can get through the next few weeks without losing my mind. Be honest with me, and take care of yourself. If you need help, ask for it. If you need someone killed because they made you mad or hurt you in some way, let me know, and I'll handle it."

I laughed until I realized he was serious, then I could only grin at him. "Deal. I'll call you as soon as I'm done."

He got up and headed toward the door. "Do you want anything from the market?"

"Tevan Summer Fruit if they have it." The rare treat was a delicacy, as the Tevan summers only lasted ten days at most. The sudden frost directly after that point made them especially sweet.

"I'll see if they do. Be careful."

I nodded to him, and he left, giving me just thirty minutes to get ready. I really hated having to rush through my usual routine, which normally took me close to forty minutes, but spending the extra stolen time with Emmanuel had been worth it.

CHAPTER
TWENTY-ONE

WITH MY hair still wet from the shower and my sheets all neat and clean, I put my com back on my wrist and called Emmanuel.

"Hey," he said, his voice warm.

I smiled up at the ceiling as I lay back on the bed. I was tired and a bit sore, but the only thing I absolutely needed was him. "Hi. I'm all done so...."

"I'll be right there. Are you in your room?"

I liked the urgency in his voice. "Yes."

He was back with me no more than ten minutes later. We lay together on the bed with his forearm under my head as a pillow and his arm around my stomach as he held me against his chest and I slowly ate my summer fruit. I savored each impossibly sweet bite and grudgingly shared a little with him each time he leaned over my shoulder, silently asking for some.

"Thank you for the treat," I said as I finished the fruit and licked my fingers clean.

He gave me a sideways squeeze, all comfort and affection. "You're welcome. Did you miss me while I was gone?"

"Yes." My client hadn't been mean or anything like that, but he was nothing like Emmanuel, and I'd wanted him back the instant he'd left my room. "Did you?"

"When I wasn't thinking about coming back here and blasting him with a neutralizer gun, yes, I did. Probably even during that time too."

The image his words put into my mind had me laughing softly beside him. "I'm glad you didn't. Monroe doesn't like our clients getting attacked while they're here. Not unless they're trying to kidnap or kill me anyway."

Emmanuel kissed the back of my head. I was about to turn toward him for a real kiss when I got a comcall. "Hello?" I said, answering the call but not bothering to put the earbud into my ear.

"Hey. Monroe tells me you're in love. Tell me everything. Is he a client? Is he going to whisk you away from your life of debauchery now?"

I rolled my eyes at my brother's antics. "Emmanuel, meet Thierry, my little brother. Thierry, Emmanuel is here. And you're on speaker. Play nice."

Thierry laughed loudly. "I am nice. I'm always nice. You, on the other hand, have been keeping secrets. So.... Emmanuel, how did you two meet?"

That was.... I frowned, not sure how Em was going to answer that question.

"I was given a contract and came to Asiq to kill him," Emmanuel replied, completely deadpan and honest.

Or, of course, the complete truth would be fine too. I cringed, not even being able to begin to guess how Thierry was going to take that bit of news. My brother started laughing, but with no one else joining in, he quickly fell silent. "Seriously? You tried to kill my big brother?"

"I did." Emmanuel didn't sound ashamed of that fact, or even sorry for it. I moved closer to him, until there was no more space between us. Thierry went off on him, but I wasn't listening anymore. Thierry had a right to be upset, of course he did, but Em trying to kill me was so far in the past that I wasn't even thinking about it anymore. He hadn't even been the most recent person to try to do so.

"Thierry—Hey. Calm down."

My words seemed to have gotten through to my brother because suddenly his angry tirade, and whatever he'd been trying to accomplish with it, were cut off. "What?" he huffed at me. "And why too? I wasn't done yelling at Emmanuel."

I bit back my laughter at Thierry's irritated tone. But I couldn't do anything for my smile. "I know. But everything is okay now."

145

"I'd die before I let anything happen to Corbin," Emmanuel added into the silence of Thierry's apparent disbelief.

I believed Em, and someday I knew Thierry would see he was telling the truth too. Maybe not right that second, but someday.

"Well that changes absolutely nothing," Thierry snapped, sounding far more like the little kid I'd sent off to go be a pilot. Well, he hadn't really been a child. He'd already been in love with Monroe in his first few months there. I shook my head, remembering my own anger when I'd found that out and knew it was his turn to be angry now.

I rolled over in Emmanuel's arms so that I could look up at him. "I want you to meet him." I could have been talking to my brother, but with my gaze fixed on Emmanuel, I was pretty sure we both knew I meant him. He stroked the back of his knuckles down my side, and I shivered lightly in his hold.

"Are you cold?" Em asked me.

Shaking my head, I brought my arm up to his shoulder. "Thierry, I need to go."

"Fine."

He sounded like a petulant child, but I could hear the smile in his words. "I'll say hi to Monroe for you."

This time he was laughing. "I'm about to go have a vidchat with him so I'll tell him myself. Thanks, though. Emmanuel, be good to my brother. Miss you, Corbin."

"I miss you too. Come back soon. Take care." I hung up on him and pulled the com off my wrist as Emmanuel turned and settled himself between my thighs. Pinned down to the bed as I was at one time might have made me feel trapped, or possibly even suffocated. I'd dealt with that and more for my clients over the years. With Em, though, I only felt comfortable and somehow safe.

I put my arms easily around his shoulders, their position already becoming familiar to us both as he leaned down and kissed me. "I don't have much more time."

"I know. I don't either. Clients to see…." There was still hurt in his eyes, and I knew it wouldn't go away overnight. But I hoped he

146

learned to trust me in time. And that I could prove to him how much better things could be between us when I was no longer having sex at Asiq with anyone but him. "I'll make sure I get rid of those clients you don't want me to have as quickly as possible. I don't want to hurt you, and I don't like that I'm doing it right now."

He laid his forehead against mine, and I closed my eyes, simply letting myself be with him without needing to do anything more as his warm breath brushed over my lips. "I know. I'm trying my best not to kidnap you and tell Monroe he can't ever have you back." The seriousness in his voice made me chuckle. "But you wouldn't be happy being with a bounty hunter."

"No more so than you would be with me knowing what I'm doing and who I'm with," I agreed with him.

"Was it hard for you to decide not to have sex with them?" he asked.

That was a difficult question for me to answer, and I took a few moments to figure out exactly what I wanted to say to him. "Not hard, not exactly anyway. I was worried Monroe wouldn't have a use for me if I couldn't perform sexual acts for my clients. Many of my clients I adore and some I think of as friends that I have while I'm here. I've had dozens of different jobs, but this is the only one I've ever felt like I was great at. And it's the only one I ever really enjoyed doing."

He was quiet for a long time as we lay together on my bed. "Do you resent me for making you give it all up?"

I heard the worry, the uncertainty in his voice, and it made me smile. "No. Not at all. And you aren't making me do anything. You told me what you wanted, and we came up with a compromise that works for both of us. I'm keeping my favorite clients, and if you can convince Resan to work with you here, then I'll have you all the time. If he refuses, then…." I didn't want to think about that possibility, but I knew I had to. "If he absolutely does not want to work here, then I'll worry about you all the time."

"I won't be able to stop thinking about you either," he promised.

"You better not."

With a groan he lifted himself up, and I let my arms fall lazily back down to the bed beside me. He didn't look like he wanted to go, which was some consolation, but I absolutely did not want to say good-bye to him again either.

"How far do you have to go to talk to Resan?" I sat up and pulled my legs under me, getting comfortable as I watched him gather up his things and get himself organized again.

Emmanuel glanced at me as he checked his guns before putting them in their holsters on either of his hips. "Resan is never more than a comcall away, and I'll talk to him once I'm out in space again. That's not why I'm leaving you right now."

I frowned and slid off the bed to be able to say good-bye to him properly instead of just waving at him. And I wanted to walk him out of Asiq as well. Part of it was being polite. The rest of my decision was based on a very primal need quite simply to let every other aspasian in Asiq know that the hot Nafsu bounty hunter on my arm was all mine.

"Then why? A job?" My guess had been correct, and he gave me a nod as he finished zipping up his jacket and straightening it over his stomach. I liked that it was tight, showing off years of well-built muscle. But I also knew it was lightly armored as well, giving him at least a little protection while he was away from me. "Anything dangerous?"

It didn't feel as strange as it once had to talk about what he did with him. He went out, and he killed people, but I stayed here, and I had sex with people too. But he was only dangerous to bad people, and I would no longer be having sex with anyone but him. They were small differences, but they did matter.

"Not really. Old man hurting children."

I nodded at the underlying anger in his voice. "Is that the job you were on Wish getting?"

"Not quite. I got another one while I was here, but I was able to find out some more information on this man. I don't often enjoy what I do, but I will take my time with him."

There was a ferocity about him in that moment, and as much as I was sure he was going to hurt the person he was going after, I could only love him a little more because of what I heard in him. "Thank you."

Emmanuel blinked down at me as if I was bordering on insanity. "For what?"

I ran my hand down his arm and tangled my fingers up in his. "There are some people in this universe who need to be out of it, as quickly as possible. And then there are people like you who make that happen. I'm saying thank you for being one of those people."

He blushed and leaned down to brush our lips together. "For a little while longer at least."

I faltered in my conviction that I always wanted him to be close, to know that he was always safe. If he was with me on Wish, then he couldn't be out there in space helping to rid the universe of bad people. But he'd be safe, and I'd always be able to see him.

"Do you enjoy what you do?"

He gave me a slow nod, as if I'd somehow judge him poorly for finding any kind of joy in what he did. If he expected that from me, we needed to have a much longer talk than we had time for currently. "Do you want to give it up?"

I waited patiently for his answer, knowing in my heart what it would be.

"I want to be able to see you more often. I want to be close to you and not have to worry about you," Emmanuel finally said.

But that wasn't an answer, not really anyway. That was a half-truth, something meant to placate me and make everything okay, without actually giving anything away. "I want that too. But I don't want you to give up something important to you either."

"You gave up sex with random people," he reminded me, as if that was the same thing as what I'd asked him to do. As if the two choices were even in the same galaxy.

I moved my hands to the waist of his pants. "I compromised. I'm still an aspasian, still in the job I love in the place I feel best in. You're giving up being a bounty hunter entirely if you join me here."

"I offered, though," he reminded me. "Because I love you."

"I love you too. But you shouldn't have to give up something important to you in order to be with me."

I didn't know what I was saying and didn't even like my words either. But I knew I needed to be fair to him, and if that meant not seeing him every day, then that's what I'd do. I loved him too much to put him into a life he only tolerated and, I feared, would eventually grow to resent.

"We'll talk when I get back," he promised.

Nodding, I knew we would. And there was one bright spot to the fear that raced through my veins as I took his hand and began leading him out of Asiq; he loved me, and I knew I would get him to come back to me in some way. It might not have been every day, but I'd have him in my life in a way I was sure would work for both of us.

CHAPTER
TWENTY-TWO

TWO DAYS later I felt someone watching me as I hung out in the lounge with clients and other aspasians. I was working on letting another of my clients go, as gently as I could, and having him in the lounge was far more comfortable for me than being yelled at by a sobbing, blubbering, irate man as I had been earlier that morning by another of my clients. I had so many regulars, which had always been a source of pride for me. But now I wished I could send them all a mass note to let them know I'd be transferring them to other aspasians, and if they could please not contact me again, that would be great. Life where people were involved didn't work like that, though, and instead I found myself listening to yet another man ask me what he did wrong that made me no longer want to see him, all while feeling someone boring holes into the back of my neck from somewhere behind me.

"You didn't do anything wrong, Alim," I promised him, reaching to put my hand on his knee in the most comforting way I could without being sexual at all. "This is a choice I'm making for myself as my life changes, and I need to start making choices to reflect that change."

He sniffled a little before his small cries built into something much more embarrassing, for both of us. "But you'll still be in Asiq?"

"Yes. I won't be going anywhere. We can still sit and have a drink together, just like we are now. But I won't be taking anyone to my bedroom again." I'd already decided that all client meetings would take place in my office, where there was no bed at all, just in case anyone thought to put me in a position where my rules for myself might be tested. They wouldn't get that chance, and I wouldn't be cheating on Emmanuel, but it was also safer for me to do this my way.

"Okay," he said, slowly coming back to himself instead of looking like I'd broken his heart. He'd only been a regular for a few months, but I'd seen him half a dozen times in that short span

"Thank you for your understanding. I'm sure you'll be quite happy with Ohra. He's a wonderful person, and he'll treat you well." I rose to my feet and gently kissed him on his cheek before I turned to see who was still staring at me.

Emmanuel gave me a slight nod when my gaze caught his, and he straightened up from where he'd been leaning against the wall across from me. Someone had given him a drink, and though I was glad he'd been taken care of while I'd been occupied, I still felt the pinch of jealousy boil up within me that someone else had done what I was supposed to do since Em was mine.

"Hey," I said, once I'd weaved my way around everyone between us. Some stood, others danced, most of them, though, lay stretched out in the lounge chairs, relaxing together and making small talk in the late morning hours when Asiq was least busy. Monroe might have been running a bed and breakfast for eunuchs for all the trouble we were getting into right then.

Emmanuel gave me a little smile, but his attention had been transferred to the man I'd been talking to now that I was by Em's side. "Letting another regular go?"

I nodded and leaned into his embrace as he wrapped one of his arms around me. His touch was gentle, and he kept his hold on me loose, as if we were affectionate friends rather than two men in love. I was glad of that since the client I'd just told I couldn't have sex with anymore was watching us just as closely as Em was scrutinizing him.

"Do they all cry?" Em asked, looking away from him.

"Mostly. Sometimes they beg too. Doesn't sound all that different from what you do."

I got him to smile at that. "I thought about what you said," he slowly began. "About me staying a bounty hunter."

He didn't need to remind me. I remembered what I'd said to him well enough on my own. It had only been a few days before, and I'd been anxiously awaiting his answer ever since. "And?" I held my breath as fear and uncertainty welled up inside me.

"Can we go somewhere to talk where we aren't surrounded by people?" he asked me instead of giving me the answer I sought.

"Of course." Going somewhere far more private would be a good idea. "Follow me."

As if this was simply a business meeting and not me finding out whether or not the man I loved would be hanging around full time, I led the way down the hallway I was sure would have been familiar to him by now. Only we didn't stop in front of my old door, as he obviously expected us to when he slowed his steps. I smiled at him and crooked my finger, leading him farther into Asiq. I stopped at a cream-colored door with a frosted glass inlay, which took up most of the wood. "This is my office. You're the first person besides myself and Monroe to be allowed in since I won't be officially starting my duties until after the last of my sexual clients has been passed off to someone else."

He gave me a little smile, though he did look nervous while doing it for whatever reason. I didn't think he had anything to be worried about. "I'd like to see it."

I smiled at him and slipped my hand into his as I opened the door and let him in. My office was much like Monroe's, with a big desk and two chairs taking up much of the room. A bedroom and a full bathroom lay through the open door to my left. But unlike Monroe's, my rooms were all furnished with light colors, and my walls were painted the same cream as my door. I had no windows, but with all the brightness inside my office, I didn't miss the lack of light.

"It's nice. I like the colors," Emmanuel said, closing the door behind himself. He locked it as well, making me grin at him as I went over to the desk and sat on top of it.

"Thanks. I do too. So...." I licked my lips. "What did you decide?" I couldn't wait any longer. I had to know his answer.

He moved between my legs, holding me close to him even before he slid me over the table until my thighs were wrapped around him. I crossed my ankles behind him and leaned back on my hands to look up at him as I waited to hear what he'd say.

"I spoke to Monroe." Which was news to me since Monroe certainly hadn't said anything the past few times I'd seen him. Even when we'd all had breakfast together that morning, he hadn't said one word of anything to me.

"And?" I prompted him, my impatience growing.

He lifted his hand to my cheek and stroked his fingers down the side of my face. "And he and I came to a compromise now that Resan is on board with also working here. Nearly all of the time we will both be here. But my reputation being as it is, people know to send me information about the bad people in the universe, like the man I hunted down yesterday. I don't relish killing, but I do enjoy making the universe safer for everyone, and killing him helped me do that."

"I agree. Making sure he didn't hurt another child was a good choice. It was a good kill." I brought my hands to his stomach and hoped he would explain the rest of what he wanted to say to me, since I could so easily tell that there was far more going on here than what he had said already.

"Monroe agrees that some people shouldn't be allowed to live and that by letting them continue to do so, even when we know what they've done and what they continue to be capable of, it is as if we are giving permission for it to continue. As if we are just as guilty for their crimes as they are since we sit here in our complacency."

I hadn't ever thought it if like that, but he did make sense, and I saw no reason to argue with him or even stop him from continuing while he spoke. I only touched him, silently encouraging him to tell me everything he wanted to.

"Monroe believes it would be best for Resan and me to continue to hunt down those people who fall into that category. When someone is brought to my attention that fits that description, I am to bring the information to Monroe for evaluation. We will talk about it, then decide together, with Resan, if this is someone he and I need to go after ourselves, or if we can trust the matter to be handled by someone else."

I breathed a heavy sigh of relief. "Thank you."

"I will still be a killer," he warned me.

That didn't bother me at all. "Yes, but you'll be my killer. And I'll only have to worry about you sometimes. The rest of the time you'll be safe, with me, here on Asiq while you and Resan watch over everyone and make sure we don't get into trouble."

"Is that satisfactory to you?"

It was more than that. The compromise was perfect. "Yes. Are you all right with that decision as well?"

He slowly nodded and ran his hands down my chest, laying me back against my empty desk. "It is. I always want to be close to you, I'll never stop wanting that, but I also wanted to be able to go after the people who cause the most harm. If I got those messages but wasn't able to do anything about them...." He shook his head, and I could plainly see how much not being allowed to right the world, even in one small way, would have hurt him.

I covered his hands on my hips with my own. "You're a good man, Em."

"I'm a killer," he reminded me, in case I'd forgotten.

I rolled my eyes instead of acknowledging that again. "How long do I have you until?"

"Monroe wants me to be ready to stand guard in the lounge at two. That gives us a few hours."

It wasn't enough time for much, but I made the most of it as I reached up and began undressing him.

RIGHT AT two he was positioned in the lounge, watching over us all. Resan stood opposite him, and together they had the full view of the large room. I smiled at him as I worked behind the bar and made a fruit smoothie for him and another for Resan.

"Arin, take this to Resan please," I told the boy in front of me who was playing with his nails.

He looked up at me as if he didn't even know who I was talking about, which was strange because I'd thought Resan had enjoyed nearly everyone in Asiq by then. Maybe Arin was too young for him, being just old enough to come into a place like Asiq. He was at least a year younger than Thierry had been when I'd first brought him to the brothel, and Arin looked just as terrified being here as Thierry had been.

"See the Sythe over there?" I nodded to Resan. Arin was Denobelas and so quite capable of producing the dark blush that suddenly stained his cheeks. "Take this drink to him. And don't be nervous around him. He's here to protect us all, not screw you as soon as you get within ten feet of him."

I'd thought joking with him would make Arin calm down a little and relax, but I'd only succeeded in making him blush even harder. Sighing, I shook my head as I watched him walk over to Resan with faltering steps to extend the drink carefully out to him. Resan, in all his usual good graces, looked simply amused as he took the drink and watched Arin scurry away from him to make himself busy talking to another aspasian.

I brought the other drink to Em and stayed beside him as he took his first sip. "How are things?"

"You mean in the hour since I last had you under me?" he quietly replied, much too low for anyone else to hear us.

I grinned. "Yes. Since then. Anything get blown up? Anyone need killing?"

"Not yet. But if that changes, I'll let you know. Promise."

I turned away from everyone else as I blew him a kiss and played with the zipper of his jacket. "You better." He shared a smile with me, and I went back to working behind the bar, where Monroe had put me for the rest of the afternoon. I mixed drinks, smiled at everyone, made small talk with anyone who came close enough to me, and was generally happy. The bright spot, though, more than anything else, was getting to have Emmanuel within five feet of me as we smiled at each other and tried to be professional while we were in view of everyone.

CHAPTER
TWENTY-THREE

ALL THOUGHTS of being professional with him went out the window around nine that night when we were in my office, and I finally had him to myself. He seemed as eager as I was because, as soon as the lock turned in the door behind us and we were officially alone, he began reaching for my clothes.

"Strip," he told me, his voice holding an air of danger. I smiled at him and slowly began taking off my shirt, exposing just a few inches of skin at a time. "Faster," he told me, followed by a growl of impatience that made me laugh.

I wasn't laughing for long, though, as he pulled my shirt over my head but not off my arms, instead pinning them behind me with the thin material. He was so fast he made me gasp, and I easily got to my knees in front of him. He brought himself closer to me, letting me see how his erection strained against his fly. I tilted my head and began licking at the thick material, running my tongue along his zipper.

His moans were soft whispers against my ears that I loved to hear. He brought his hands to my hair, tangling his long fingers with my dark strands. "Take me out. With your mouth. Don't move your hands."

This was a new side of him that I hadn't had before, and I found myself absolutely loving having him take control of me so easily. I wanted to please him, to show him staying here with me and for me, was the right choice for him to make. I needed him to know that.

I was able to free his cock with little difficulty, and he dipped his hips to feed himself between my lips. I covered my teeth and looked up at him, finding joy in simply being with him, in loving him however he wanted me to. He smiled down at me and ran his fingers through my hair, letting my long hair fall over my shoulders.

"You are so unbelievably beautiful," he whispered to me, his voice hoarse with pleasure. I thought he'd stop there, with his compliment coiled tightly in my heart where I kept it safe, along with all the others he'd ever given to me. They were precious to me, and I never wanted to let them go. But then he continued. "I wish I knew what I did to deserve you. What I could do to keep you with me. Always."

I pulled away, instantly missing the feeling of having him between my lips, but I needed to be able to speak too. This was too important to simply let go and brush aside, to ignore for now and talk about later. "You don't have to worry about me going away, Em. Not ever. I love you. All of you. The fierce killer, the protector, the man who will do anything to keep me safe. The one who loves me, who can be gentle with me one moment, then pull out his neutralizer the next in order to protect me. I'll always love you."

I didn't know what else to say or what more to do to get him to see that. I could only hope someday he understood and believed me.

"I don't think I deserve you, though," he whispered to me, his voice breaking.

I gave him a sad little smile. "I feel the same way."

He chuckled, and believing we were fine for the moment, I leaned forward and slipped my lips around his head again. I went slowly, wanting to show him how much I loved him. I was gentle, with none of my usual speed as I rushed to get the guy I was with off as quickly as possible. This was me being gentle with Emmanuel, me showing him how much I loved him, how desperately I wanted him in my life.

When his head pressed against the back of my throat and his hips bucked into my mouth, I swallowed him down. I sighed around his base and lapped up every drop as he leaned over me, his hands on my shoulders, holding me against him. He'd supported me as I'd loved him with my mouth.

Em shakily straightened back up, but I didn't release his softening cock until he moved away from me. And then I simply watched him. "I can't believe you love me," he told me, going to his knees in front of me.

I smiled at him and leaned forward. Without the use of my hands, I expected him to catch me before I fell forward, and he didn't disappoint me in the least as he pulled me forward the rest of the way and rested my head on his shoulder. "I can't believe you were going to shoot me."

Em laughed and ran his hands down my arms. "I'm glad I didn't."

"Me too."

Leaning against him was comfortable, but I still needed attention too. "Em?"

"Yes?"

I smiled into his shoulder. "I'd like to get off too."

He kissed the side of my head. "Of course. How do you—?"

"With your hand, just like this," I said, interrupting him.

With my shirt away from my chest, he had free access to my nipples, which he took full advantage of as soon as he turned my head to face him. His kisses were soft at first, tentative, just like his fingers around my nipples as he teased and played with me. But as soon I released my first startled gasp, he added his nails to the mix, sending fire racing through my open nerves.

Em slipped his tongue between my teeth, and I eagerly sucked on him as he moved his hand lower. I was panting into his mouth before he even undid the drawstring to my pants. He didn't pull them off. There wasn't need. He only had enough room to get his hand in, but it seemed that was all he wanted as he kept my mouth on his and eagerly took me into his hand. He stroked me quickly, pulling me toward him as he took control of me.

Sanity quickly slipped away from me as I flamed. I didn't need to think, only to feel, and with him holding me, supporting me, and taking care of me as he was, I didn't question anything else. I was safe, protected, and completely out of control of myself. I had no reason to worry. I didn't even think about it. I couldn't have formed a coherent thought right then if I'd suddenly had to. Not having to, though, that was the bliss of it. I cried out against his mouth when I came, and he quickly swallowed down the sound as I jerked against his palm.

Em laid me down on my side, my cheek resting against his thigh. I'd made a mess of his hand, but he acted like it didn't matter to him at all as he rested it near my face. I curled onto my side, getting even more comfortable against him as I moved forward. He didn't move his hand away from me as I started to lick him clean, and when I looked up at him, I saw him smiling down at me.

"Will you get tired of me telling you how beautiful you are?"

"Unlikely," I replied as I sucked his thumb gently between my teeth. Without the fury of my need driving my actions, I became lazy as I lapped at his fingers, cleaning them off as slowly as I wanted to. There was no reason to rush.

He stroked his free hand down my cheek. "You are, though. Always, but especially like this, when you're obviously enjoying yourself."

I turned over onto my back, now reasonably sure that his hand was clean of my come. "The first time I thought you were really stunning was when you were above me in my bed back at the station." Having my hands trapped behind me put me at an odd angle, but I didn't mind it too much as I relaxed into the feeling of his hands trailing lightly over my skin as he explored my chest with featherlight touches.

"I was worried, and so nervous," he confided. "You've been with so many men, I didn't know how to compare to them. How to show you what little I knew how to do."

Smirking, I shook my head, then opened my eyes to look back up at him. "You never had to think that you needed to compare yourself to any of them. You blew them all away by simply loving me."

"I promise that I will always love you. For as long as I'm alive." He blushed and dragged his fingertips up my chest, making

160

me arch against his touch. "Are you comfortable like that? You don't look like it."

"I'm really not. Can I move my hands now?" He gave me a blank look, and I grinned up at him. "You told me not to."

"Sorry. Yes, of course you can." He helped me get my hands free of my shirt, and I rolled my shoulders without getting off his knees. Crossing my hands over my navel was a much more comfortable position. "I'm sorry. I didn't realize you were waiting for me to tell you it was okay to move them."

"Don't worry about it," I quickly reassured him. "I was pretty comfortable overall until I decided to roll onto my back, and I do like a bit of kink sometimes. You may feel free to tie me up anytime. Ordering me around works too."

"I'd like that. I like seeing you on your knees and watching my shaft go between your lips." He confessed that as if it was some big, dark secret only I was allowed to know. I thought he was amazingly adorable. And he was still sexy too, but there was something completely sublime about being able to have this side of Emmanuel all to myself, the one where he wasn't completely sure of himself and he wasn't ready to jump into battle, but simply loved me.

CHAPTER
TWENTY-FOUR

THE FIRST test of our new reality came a week later when Resan came to my office door and knocked loudly. Emmanuel was in my office, but we weren't exactly doing work, and I was quick to straighten my clothes and get off my knees before answering the door. I hoped I didn't look completely obvious, but by Resan's smirk, it was pretty clear that I'd failed to fix some part of me that gave away what we'd been doing.

"Your chin is dirty," he told me as he stepped past me and into my office.

I wiped at it and instantly felt wetness against my fingers. "Of course it is," I grumbled to myself, and quickly licked my fingers clean. Em looked completely composed, as if we'd been discussing what we would be having for lunch. I wanted to know his secret.

"A call came in. New job," Resan explained as he handed his holoscreen over to Em for him to read too. I could have hung back and let the bounty hunters do their thing and not interfere with them. That wasn't really my style, though, and I walked over to Em's shoulder to read too.

Resan said nothing as Em slid the holoscreen over to me to scan as well. Reading about the man's crimes against women didn't even compare to the pictures I shouldn't have scrolled down to see. I handed the holoscreen back to Resan with shaking fingers. He put it away, and I looked up at Em. "Be careful and kill him a lot." I put my hand on Em's forearm, needing his support right then. I worried about him going up against someone like that, but I knew he was strong, and

Resan was fast. They would protect each other and made an excellent team out there.

"Monroe still needs to okay us going."

"He will." I was confident about that. He cared about people as much as I did and wouldn't let this man's actions slide if he could do something about it. And, I realized, now he could. He had a bounty hunter and a peacekeeper available to him. "You'll be careful? Both of you?"

Resan looked surprised, as if he didn't think I'd include him in that order. "I'll make sure Emmanuel comes back to you in one piece."

I shook my head and touched his arm as well with my free hand. "I meant that you needed to be careful too, Resan. Use actual, deadly guns. Not neutralizers. Don't be stupid. And kill him."

Em kissed my forehead, then tried to walk away, but that wasn't good enough for me. Letting go of Resan, I grabbed Em in a tight hug and lifted myself up on the tips of my toes to kiss him as he was supposed to have kissed me. It was a real kiss, not the light peck on my forehead he'd tried to get away with. Breathless after the kiss, I stepped back. "When you leave for a job, you kiss me like that. Forehead when we're in front of everyone, but Resan knows us well enough that I get a real kiss, even when he's around."

Laughing, Em nodded to me. "Sure. Deal."

He started heading toward the door, but Resan hadn't moved from in front of my desk. "Do I get a kiss too?"

I rolled my eyes. "I'll give you a kick in your dick if you try it." But I did walk up to him and gave him a light hug. He returned the gesture, though a bit awkwardly, then they were off to see Monroe.

WHILE EM was gone, I worried about him every day. I couldn't help it. And none of the sector news was helpful in letting me know if he was okay or not. I didn't even know if he was in the sector at all to begin with, so I might have been completely unable to find out anything. I still listened to the news feeds and read any report that came through my inbox, though, desperate to find out anything I could about Em and how he and Resan were doing. I knew having them go away would be hard. But I hadn't expected to pace back and forth and jump every time my com lit up with a new call.

Thierry had been a bit of a distraction, but I didn't feel fine again until Em joined me in bed a week later. I'd been completely asleep, the time being well after midnight, but as soon as I felt the bed dip behind me, I was wide-awake and turning on the light to see Em fully.

He didn't give me a chance to comment on his bruises as he lay over me, sliding between my thighs. It was always summer on Wish, always hot, and I'd gone to bed naked. With him rubbing against me, I knew that would quickly become the norm. "Are you hurt?" I asked him when he stopped kissing me long enough to let me take a breath.

"Bruised but nothing broken. I'm completely able to enjoy you," he promised. I hadn't been thinking about having sex with him, but I believed that he was telling me the truth, and my body was instantly responding to the sweet friction of having him naked and pressing against me.

"I tried to call you," I said as he pulled some lubricant out of the bedside drawer and slicked it over his fingers. Being stretched for him took no time at all as relaxing with him nearby came naturally to me by then.

He kissed the side of my neck as I panted in time with his fingers as he stroked them into my hole. "I know. I was slightly busy killing someone."

"Next time you answer. I was worried."

He chuckled and took my mouth in a rough kiss as he replaced his fingers with the blunt head of his cock. He tightened his hands around my waist, and I slid one of my knees up his shoulder, giving him a better angle into me. His first thrust took him to the base, and I groaned against the pain, against the burning, against everything that wasn't the sheer tangled mess of pleasure Em quickly began to build inside me with each hard thrust. Being with him was wonderful, knowing he was safe and back in my arms was bliss, but I especially enjoyed the primal way he took me as he plowed into my hole. He fucked me as if he realized I wouldn't break. As if he knew that I'd tell him the second something he did hurt me or didn't feel amazing.

I needed that kind of trust from him, and he seemed like he needed it too as he shot wave after wave of pure heat and bliss through me. He grunted in my ear and bit me on my neck, and I loved every hard, wonderful second of it until the feeling of him rubbing against the underside of my cock with each of his thrusts became too much for me.

I crashed over that wave, fell below it as my pleasure took hold of me and pulled me down deep. There was nothing else in the room, no bed, no obnoxiously bright lights, just Em and me as I came, shouted his name, and dug my fingers so hard into his shoulders, I was sure he'd have all new bruises there in the morning.

He jerked into me a few seconds later, then went completely still. Sweaty and sated, he fell on top of me, and I welcomed his weight as he crushed me into the bed.

"Fuck," I gasped when words, and somewhat full thoughts, had come back to me.

Emmanuel laughed breathlessly and slid away from me. I missed his contact and quickly joined him across the bed, lying against him as he curled onto his side and tucked me into the bed in front of him. I felt his softening head against me as he brought his arms around me, keeping me close and tight against him.

"For the record, my plan was to let you sleep and have you in the morning. You weren't supposed to wake up."

I snorted and shook my head. That was a stupid plan. "When you come back, whether you're gone for a day or a week, no matter what time it is or what else I'm doing, you bring me in here, and you take me. End of story. I need you when you're gone, and I have to have you the second you're back. That's the plan and the rule. Nothing else."

"Even if you're in a meeting with Monroe?"

I nodded, and Em kissed the back of my head. "Yes. He'll understand. He's an adult who has sex with my little brother. He'll get over anything he has to, to deal with for me to be able to get you naked immediately."

He laughed, and I loved him a little more for that, as if there was any room left in me to find any more love for him. I felt like I was overflowing all the time already. He threaded his fingers through mine on the bed. "I'll always be yours," he promised.

"And I'm yours too."

He leaned forward and pressed his forehead against the back of my head. I felt his warm breaths against the back of my neck, right at the top of my spine, and I smiled as I closed my eyes. I hadn't slept well while he'd been gone, but I knew I could get a few hours now that he was back. I had to be awake at seven, which only gave me a little while to sleep beside him, but that was enough.

He turned away from me for a second, and I groaned in protest. I was too comfortable to be disturbed like that, and I closed my eyes tightly against his movements, willing him to stay still. My eyes flew open a second later, though, as he pressed something warm and circular into my palm.

"Em?" I asked him as I looked from the shiny metal band back to him over my shoulder.

"Please?" he asked me, as simply as that. All his hopes, all his dreams, and every fear that I'd reject him was so obvious in that one word that it took me a few seconds to remember how to speak as I simply turned to stare at him over my shoulder.

"Yes," I said, letting him slide the ring over my left ring finger. It was loose, at first, before it tightened around me. It was still somehow impossibly warm, which was a comfort to me. "I love you."

"I love you too. Thank you."

He sounded sleepy now, and I said nothing more as I leaned back against him until there was no space left between us. There didn't need to be any either. This was perfect. We'd always be together, and he would always be mine. I smiled one more time as I looked down at my new ring and closed my eyes. I was ready to go to sleep now as I let myself drift off into fantasies of what being married to Em would be like. We'd have quiet dinners and evenings just like this, where clothes were the only thing not allowed.

Stay tuned for an excerpt from

To the Highest Bidder

A Planet Called Wish:
Book One

By Caitlin Ricci

The Intergalactic Star Pilot Academy has accepted Thierry Leroux into the elite class of sky year 2231. But the academy comes with a hefty price tag, and there's no way he, a poor Sythe orphan, has the credits the academy requires. Thierry's brother, Corbin, a high-class companion, suggests Thierry sell his virginity for the cost of tuition. It seems like a ridiculous idea, but it may be Thierry's only shot, so Thierry asks Corbin to arrange a meeting on the pleasure planet of Wish.

On Wish, Thierry meets Corbin's boss, Monroe, and they agree to auction off Thierry's virginity. Thierry is grateful to the masked buyer he knows only as "Dragonfly," and Dragonfly is gentle, making Thierry's first time a good memory. When Dragonfly requests to see him again, and pay for the pleasure, Thierry returns to Wish. But in this game, falling in love is dangerous for the heart, and Thierry might not like the man behind the mask.

CHAPTER
ONE

I GLANCED up from the holoscreen I held as the warning indicator flashed high on the wall across from me. The blinking red light continued for a few minutes as the shuttle docked and the air lock closed outside the apartment I shared with my brother. There was a less direct way of getting home, by docking at the actual station port a few levels up, but for a shuttle as small as his, he could hook up right outside the living room and come right in. Not everyone in the station had an apartment that backed to space, but Corbin liked the convenience of simply being able to dock and then being home. And he paid the bills so I went with it. As the light switched off, the front door slid open and the automatic doorbell rang, along with a loud mechanical voice announcing my brother's return home.

"Hey," I called, moving my sore muscles enough to force myself to sit up on the couch I'd been lying on most of the afternoon while I read. The holoscreen slowly went dim from my inattention as my brother locked the automatic door behind him.

"Damn, I'm exhausted," Corbin said, plunking down on the couch beside me. Though my brother made the claim, he certainly didn't look it. Two weeks away appeared to have done well for him. His purple skin shone with a faint gold undertone, and his eyes had a sheen that had not been there when I'd last seen him.

"Business was good?" I asked, even though I was already guessing the answer from my brother's easy, definitely satisfied grin.

He ruffled my short hair and leaned back, resting his head on the couch. His long black hair fell over the back of it, nearly touching the floor. He closed his eyes, and for a moment I thought he wasn't going to answer me, but then my brother dug a hand into the pocket of his loose black slacks and pulled out a clear tube of credit crystals. My eyes went wide, and I reached for the container, but Corbin quickly pulled it out of my reach.

"Uh-uh, nope. This chunk is for bills. And I worked hard for it."

Coloring deeply, I nodded. "I know you did. That's a lot, though. Even after Monroe's cut?" I couldn't believe it. I knew my brother enjoyed his work, but still, that was more than I'd seen him bring home in, well, ever really.

My brother's lids lifted, revealing eyes darker than the space that lay outside our station's protective outer core. "Yeah. Monroe only takes 15 percent. And I had some great businessmen as customers this time, making a stop between planets. Wish draws all kinds, but these men were loaded. Great tippers, and my time with them wasn't half bad."

"Were they like us?" I asked eagerly, hoping to hear of these travelers who were so far outside what I knew of the world, which largely consisted of the men and women of the space station we lived on since I hardly ever got to venture off it. There was no need when everything was so conveniently brought to us. Besides, shuttle travel was expensive, and there was no reason to waste fuel.

"'Like us,' meaning Sythe?" Corbin replied, getting up and stretching his arms over his head. I nodded. "Nah, they weren't. Denobelas, the lot of them. Same as Monroe."

I sat back and said, "Oh," like I understood, even though I really didn't. I didn't know any Denobelas and had only ever seen the dominant race in hologram broadcasts. I knew they looked like the ancient race of humans that had long ago been bred out. But as Corbin had explained to me where his information holograms left off, they had their differences as well. He said it was supposedly more psychological than physical, whatever that was supposed to mean. I didn't really know what he was talking about a lot of the time when he went on about the different people he met or where he went while he was working. It all sounded so fantastic to me, this whole universe I'd barely experienced but had been hearing about for years.

"What's this?" he asked.

I was about to question what he was talking about when the message started playing. I froze, sure I'd hidden it and wishing I'd done a better job of it. Corbin wasn't supposed to find out about the message, but it wasn't like I could do anything about it now.

"Congratulations, Thierry Leroux. You've been selected for the elite class of sky year 2231. You and thirty of your best and brightest peers will have the exclusive opportunity to learn from the sharpest minds of today and tomorrow at the Intergalactic Star Pilot Academy. Your acknowledgement is expected within sixty days. Here's what you'll need to bring—"

"Turn it off," I grumbled, laid my arms over my knees, then lowered my head. I didn't need to hear the message again. I'd already memorized it the first six times I'd heard it, just to be sure I knew what they were really saying. But then I'd figured out what else was on the message. Sure, my heart had soared with the possibilities of being able to be everything I'd ever wanted. Being a star pilot had been my dream since I was three and saw one of the first shuttles land on our isolated home planet. Now, nearly two decades later, I'd never forgotten about that seemingly impossible idea of being up there among the elite few.

Corbin came back to the couch and touched my shoulder. I tried to pull away, but my brother's long fingers curled in the thin material of my shirt, keeping me still. I didn't mind the restriction to my movements, but it did mean I'd have to tell Corbin, and I wasn't sure I was really able to talk about it. At least not yet.

"You've always wanted this. Why didn't you tell me you were able to get in? That's great news." The joy was obvious in his voice, but I shook my head, dismissing his words.

"I don't want it anymore. It was a stupid dream." My voice broke on the lie. Of course I still wanted it. For years I'd pictured myself in those ships, traveling the galaxy, learning everything I could about whatever they'd hand me. I wouldn't be a captain. That wasn't something I was interested in. But a pilot was a far better opportunity, especially for a poor Sythe orphan from a tiny station that was barely large enough to need a registration number.

He shook his head, released my shirt, and stepped back, giving me some room. "No, it wasn't. Why would you ever say it was?" He crouched, staring up at me with dark eyes. I didn't understand why my brother looked so hurt, so confused. Wasn't this supposed to be my life? My dream? What did it matter if I decided not to do it anymore? Was giving up really so wrong?

"I don't want it anymore," I whispered, looking away. My brother knew too much. Years as a paid aspasian for the visitors of Wish had given him too much insight into how other people worked. That he now used that ability on me, his younger brother, wasn't in the least bit fair.

He shook his head. "Yeah, you do. How about you stop lying to me, and tell me why you've decided to give up on something you've thought about for the past fifteen years?" His black brows rose unexpectedly, and I bit my lip.

It was on the tip of my tongue to lie. But as Corbin wrapped his hand around mine, and the warmth of my brother's touch fired along my sensitive nerves, I chose the better option. The truth slipped off my tongue like acid, though I knew it was the right choice. Lying to Corbin, the only family I had left in all the universe, simply wasn't an option for me.

"We can't afford it. It's too expensive."

His lips tightened, and he released me. He sat back and crossed his legs, getting comfortable on the floor in front of me. "So that's it."

I nodded, feeling lost and like I'd somehow let myself and Corbin down.

"And they don't offer scholarships for that program, do they?"

"No," I replied, though he knew that well enough. He'd sat there with me as the head of the program talked to us, walking us through the process. Orientation had lasted three straight days, and although I had loved being in the academy, I'd never thought I had the slightest chance of getting in. My test scores were fine—it wasn't that. I just didn't have the background for it. ISPA was prestigious. Always had been. They accepted and graduated only the best in the galaxy. I'd always known I didn't register anywhere near that level.

"I'll pick something else. It's fine," I told him, hoping he would let me brush off the only dream I'd ever had as easily as I'd tried to lie to him.

He snorted and shook his head. "Yeah, no, Thierry. We're not playing that game. You're going to the academy. We'll just have to find something to sell." He frowned and looked around our tiny apartment. I didn't need to look. I'd thought about that first and hadn't found anything. I'd had a full week while Corbin was away working on Wish to think of things I could sell to make the money I needed to chase that impossible dream. "Do they take payments?" he asked hopefully.

I shook my head. "Twenty thousand credits needed up front as payment, then it's five thousand every year after the first." Even talking about that much money made my stomach cramp. Corbin made a good amount in his two weeks per month serving the wealthiest of the galaxy, but he'd never brought home that much. Before I'd received the message, I hadn't ever seen that much money required for anything. Even our shuttle had cost only a fourth of that, and Corbin had been paying that off for the last five years.

Whistling low, Corbin looked as surprised as I had been. "Wow. So that's why they didn't tell us how much their academy cost when I asked. Pricey little joint, huh?" I nodded miserably. "So for three years there, you'd need thirty thousand grams of credits."

I looked at the hologram lying on the well-worn table between us. A picture of the ISPA's front door welcomed me in. If only it were that easy. I'd never wanted anything more and couldn't believe I'd been accepted; it was so far out of my reach.

"There's nothing to sell," I quietly admitted. "It's hopeless."

He was silent for several long moments, and I was sure he hadn't heard me. But then he offered an idea that was too ridiculous to be believed. "You have yourself," he said, his voice soft as I met his dark gaze.

Now it was my turn to look shocked. My mouth fell open. "You mean be a prostitute. Like you. You want me to do that?"

Corbin rolled his eyes. "Prostitute isn't what we like to be called, little brother. I am an aspasian when I'm there. It's pretty fun. And besides, it's paid your bills for the past few years, so why knock it now?"

I nodded, realizing instantly I'd crossed the line. Corbin was proud of what he did and enjoyed his work. And he was right: it had paid our bills and bought me the clothes I was wearing. If he wasn't working on Wish, we would be homeless right now, just like we had been on our home planet.

"Sorry. You're right. I…. Sorry." I felt guilty for saying what I had and for thinking badly of my brother's chosen profession. But at the back of my mind, there was some part of me that felt wrong for considering my brother's words.

"Would you leave? You know, if you could?" I asked, looking at him.

"If I could leave? You think I'm trapped there?" my brother asked, sounding at once offended and amused. I wasn't really sure what to believe anymore now that I was actually considering this. Corbin's dark lips spread into a warm smile, one he'd often claimed brought men into his bed without any further work on his part. "I wouldn't. No. Even if I found someone and fell in love with them, I wouldn't quit my job. I love it."

"You love having sex with strangers?"

Corbin snorted. "You think that's all I do? Just lie on my back and badly fake some moans?"

And suddenly I was bright red and stuck somewhere between complete embarrassment and curiosity. The latter won out, and I simply shrugged, unsure what else to do as my brother started talking. "People come to Asiq for the fantasy. Wish is a planet covered in brothels, but there's a big difference between Asiq and the others, and that's why I work there. They're not coming to Monroe's club for a quick lay, and his prices reflect that. We're highly valued there because we give the customers the whole package. If you wanted to do this, he'd have to train you up some, but it shouldn't be too hard. I only needed a few intense days before I was ready for my first client.

We provide companionship, entertainment, and yes, when asked, we do perform sexual acts for our clients. But most of my day is not spent naked," Corbin said.

With my brother's words playing in my mind, I tried to imagine the place where my brother worked. I'd never asked, never really wanted to know what Corbin did the two weeks a month he was gone. In all honesty I'd accepted my brother's money, used it to buy food and other things we needed, but hadn't thought about it further than that. Maybe I'd been too afraid or too ashamed of what I thought my brother did for our money. Now, though, I wasn't so sure.

"Can you... um... walk me through a normal day, then?" I asked.

Corbin's brows rose. "You're really considering this, aren't you?"

"It's the only way to become a pilot, right? Smuggling would take too long. And drug running is—"

"Out of the question," Corbin snapped at me, leaning forward and catching my gaze. "Not only is that extremely dangerous, but if you're caught, there go your hopes for a future in the program anyway. So no, you're not doing that." He sighed loudly and dragged his hands through his hair. "Relax about it for now. You've got two weeks to think about what you want to do. I'll call Monroe and see what he says."

I nodded and waited as he punched buttons on the com unit attached to his wrist. "Speaker please," I whispered as he was about to put the earpiece in. Corbin complied, and a moment later the call connected.

"Miss me so soon?" an unfamiliar voice at the other end joked.

I pulled my knees up to my chest and laced my hands around my ankles. I'd never heard Monroe's voice before, but it sounded warm. What kind of man ran a brothel, especially one as successful as Asiq?

Corbin smiled. "No, old man, not yet. I've only been gone four hours. But I do have an idea for you."

"Will I like it?"

"Maybe," Corbin said, looking at me. "But right now it's only in the maybe phase. My brother had a thought."

"I'm listening."

He lifted his hand and waved me down to sit beside him. Reluctantly I went, my sore muscles from lying there too long protesting as I moved to the floor and sank onto my knees beside Corbin. "Tell him yourself," he said, his voice gentle.

"Um…." I didn't know where to begin.

"My time is valuable, Corbin, you know that. If your brother is unable to voice his needs now, perhaps you should call back later, when he is more articulate."

I swallowed thickly. I didn't know the other man at all, but I did recognize someone quickly losing their patience when I heard it. Damn. This was not how I imagined this going, not that I'd had very long to think about it before Corbin had sprung this impromptu phone call on me.

"He's thinking," Corbin quickly covered for me, but a sharp jab in my ribs told me I needed to do it much faster.

I licked my lips and leaned closer to the com unit. "Sir, I am… I'd like to…. You see…."

"Take a breath and try again," Monroe said, sounding calmer.

I tried again. "Sorry, sir. I'm a bit nervous. You see, I need to ask a favor."

There was a loud groan on the other end of the line, and I instantly felt bad for bringing it up. Of course he didn't want to hear about it. This was a stupid idea. I was an idiot for even thinking about it and wasting the other man's time.

"All right, I'm listening. You want a favor from me?"

I considered my words even as my heart raced so quickly, I thought I would pass out for sure. "I need money. Lots of it, really quickly."

Monroe chuckled. "Well, Wish is the place to make it. If you want to interview the next time your brother comes out, I'll give you one. Is that all?"

"No, you don't understand. I don't want to work for you," I quickly snapped. Then, realizing how badly that sounded, I spoke again. "I want to be a star pilot. But the academy's price tag is so far out of this galaxy, I start to feel sick just looking at it."

"So?"

I took a breath and steeled my nerves. "So I was thinking about auctioning off my virginity at Asiq." There. I'd said it. And in the silence that followed, I considered all the ways it could have gone better.

But then Monroe replied. "I would take 25 percent of the price to cover advertising and training costs."

My mouth fell open. "That's ridiculous! Corbin only gives you fifteen!"

"Yes, but your brother has been working at Asiq for years. He had a one-year contract to begin with and has extended that each year since. I've made my investment back on him. If he continues to stay, then each year after his seventh, my cut goes down until I keep just 5 percent of what he earns to cover the cost of keeping Asiq up and employing the security a place like this needs. You, on the other hand, are asking for a one-time deal. I can make it profitable for you, of that I have no doubt. Virgins are exceedingly valuable in this industry. But it will take time to train you and get the word out about what you're intending to do. So that's my offer: 25 percent."

"I don't even know if I want to do this," I grumbled, feeling foolish in light of Monroe making perfect sense. I could see the business side of things, and as little as Corbin had told me about Monroe, I at least knew he was a businessman above anything else.

"Think it over. Decide if you can handle giving yourself away to a stranger. Most people can't. I can get you the money you need for your school, but you need to decide if the price is worth it. Now, if you'll excuse me, I have some customers to take care of. Is there anything else you need, either of you?"

Corbin brought the com closer to his mouth. "No, sir. Thank you."

"And what is your brother's name?"

"Thierry," I spoke up, looking at Corbin and wishing I could give words to all the feelings swirling inside me.

"Then good-bye for now, Thierry. I'm sure we'll talk again soon."

I nodded, though Monroe couldn't see me. I'd give the man an answer either way before Corbin left again.

CHAPTER TWO

TWO WEEKS went by far too quickly, and I still didn't have an answer for Monroe. I actually half figured my brother had probably forgotten all about it in that time since neither of us mentioned it again. But as I woke up early to say good-bye to Corbin again, I knew I had to make a decision, and fast. There were too many questions, too many variables I needed to figure out, though, before I could choose a course of action and really stick with it. The letter from the academy glared at me from the holoscreen on my desk, reminding me I was quickly running out of time if I really did want to get in. There was no saving up for next year with them. If I didn't accept the position, I was done for. That was it. They didn't allow second chances. But what if I did everything Monroe said and still didn't make enough money? What then?

Could I still look myself in the mirror after selling my body?

"I'm leaving now," Corbin called from outside my bedroom door.

With a sick feeling in my gut, I opened it and looked up at my older brother, wishing Corbin could make everything right like he'd done years ago when I would have a nightmare and he'd come chase away the monsters with a song and some sweet taffy.

"What do I need to take with me?" I whispered, the words sounding choked as I forced them up and out of my throat.

Corbin looked surprised for only a moment before he quickly pushed his way into my room. My heavy duffle fell to the bed as Corbin bent down and pulled a bag out of my closet. I didn't think I'd really need two bags for the trip, but I wasn't up to arguing with him either.

"Pack your shampoo, toothpaste, razors, shaving cream, soap, and enough changes of clothes to last you two weeks. Monroe has a laundry system, but you need to have options available. And take towels," Corbin said as he began tossing the clothes he knew I liked into the bag. "Don't worry about being neat right now. We need to get going. Just get it in the bag. Food isn't necessary since Monroe feeds us well, but if you have something you absolutely can't live without, take it. Just hurry. And Thierry?"

"Yeah?"

Corbin gave me a strange look before he pulled me close. "Make sure you want to do this. If we get there and you say absolutely no, then tell Monroe. This is your choice. Always your choice. You don't do anything you don't want to. Don't let the other guys mess with you, and don't take crap from anyone there. Monroe will take care of you if you can't find me. And if you decide you don't want to do this, he will find something else for you to do during the two weeks we're there. It won't be fun, but you'll probably be cleaning or helping in the kitchen. That's what he makes the guys that have bad attitudes do anyway."

I nodded and clutched Corbin's light jacket. "Thanks."

Stepping away, Corbin smirked at me. "Never thought I'd be taking you to Wish."

I blushed. "Didn't ever really plan on going."

He ruffled my short black hair. "I've got to call Monroe and let him know what you decided. Get packed. We leave in ten."

That wasn't enough time to do much of anything, but at least I'd already gotten dressed and showered early, unlike most times when Corbin left and I was barely crawling out of bed. I quickly ran around my room, grabbing everything I thought I might need and shoving it haphazardly into the bag. With seconds to spare, I was ready to go and standing in the kitchen, my knuckles turning white as I gripped the countertop.

"I don't know if I can do this," I grumbled to myself. My stomach turned, and I put a hand on it, hoping it would calm down. I hadn't been sick on our shuttle since the first time I'd been in it and did not want to meet Monroe with vomit on my breath.

Corbin came out of his room and slung his duffle over one shoulder. "Come on if you're coming," he said, his heavy boots making loud noises on the floor as he walked. I scrambled to keep up with him, not wanting to be left behind.

"I hope Monroe likes me," I said uncertainly as I mimicked Corbin's movements and put my bag over my shoulder.

Corbin chuckled and looked over at me. "You'll be fine. Remember, you're not doing this as a career. It's a one-time event for you."

"What's that mean?" I asked him. "Will I be treated differently than the other guys?"

Opening our front door and stepping out into the shiny metallic hallway of the space station, Corbin shrugged. "Some of them might. They may think you believe you're better than them. But maybe not. Asiq isn't like the other places on Wish. You don't have to hide what you are when you come back from there." He locked the door behind me, and together we made our way down the narrow space between apartments. I could hear other people moving around in their homes, but most were still asleep this early. Corbin continued talking, though his voice was a lot quieter now that we were out in the open between levels on the space station. "I work there two weeks a month, but I'm not a whore. I don't live there, and I don't take clients outside of Asiq. That's the mentality most of the guys have. We have fun when we're at work, but we don't get paid for sex the rest of the time."

"When people ask what you do, do you tell them?" I asked as we climbed a short flight of stairs to the landing bay.

Corbin shrugged. "Depends on the person. But yeah, I usually do."

"Even the guys you're with back here?" I continued. I knew my brother dated, but he'd always been pretty careful about who he brought around me. He told me where he was going, and who with, but I hadn't met someone he'd been with in at least six months.

Corbin's black brows lifted. "Especially them. But I don't usually have quickies with strangers. That's one benefit of working at Asiq. If all I wanted was sex, there are plenty of customers and guys working there that I could get sex from. That need is easily satisfied, and Monroe doesn't stand in our way if we want to have fun with each other as long as it doesn't interfere with his business. So when I meet a guy outside of work, I don't just jump into bed with him."

I nodded, getting more insight into my brother's personal life than I had in years. It wasn't that we weren't close, I just hadn't asked. I never had. Corbin had decided to apply at Asiq, and that had been the end of it. He kept his business life private and separated from the life we had at home, and I appreciated that. But I was just now realizing how much I needed to learn about what it meant to work at Asiq if I was actually going through with this.

It was an easy walk from the floor with the apartments to where the ships were kept in the shuttle bay. Our station was small, but it was one of the few places to fuel up this far away from the central planets. The shuttle bay doors opened when Corbin put his palm on the reader, and minutes later I strapped myself into the shiny black passenger pod of Corbin's shuttle. Our bags were secured in a cabinet behind me, and Corbin sat in front, the pilot I wanted to be. Except I didn't want to fly small station-to-planet shuttles. I wanted to explore universes. And no one would give that kind of clearance to just anyone. I needed an education to get to that level.

"There's a pack of sedatives in the cargo hold beside you," Corbin called back as the clamps released the bow of the shuttle. There was jolt as our little ship was released, but it quickly smoothed out as the air lock ahead of us closed, followed by the one behind, and then Corbin was reversing our shuttle out into the little take-off area. We still weren't in open space, but it was close enough that I could see it through the thick window panels. Corbin swung us around, his movements precise and practiced after so many years of owning the ship.

"I don't need them," I replied as I folded my hands in my lap and wished I'd thought to bring a heavier jacket. I knew Corbin had on layers, and I hadn't put it together until now, when I was really shivering. I so rarely went into space I'd forgotten how cold it was away from the heated interior of the station. "Can I get some heat back here?"

A flick of a switch by my brother's side, and the cabin slowly filled with gentle warmth. It wasn't as much as I would have liked, but it was more than I'd had before. At least it was only a short ride to

Wish. Any longer than that, and I would have had more time to think about what I was getting myself into.

"Nervous?" Corbin asked once we'd been cleared to leave the station. The final set of doors closed behind us, and I looked out into open space, a slow smile forming on my lips.

I nodded. "Yes. Were you? On your first time, I mean?"

"I didn't come to Asiq as a virgin, so things were different for me. But yeah, I was nervous. This profession will get you over being self-conscious really fast. And it can be exhausting, both mentally and physically. You don't get to have off days while you're there. If you do, you're taken out of the lineup and Monroe will give you something else to do or, if you don't want to do it anymore at all, he'll cash you out then and there, and you're gone. He doesn't play around with people who don't want to be in Asiq or aren't having a good day. The customers don't come to listen to our problems."

I let his words sink in and tried to think past the lump in my stomach.

Four hours later we were landing in a bright courtyard along with other shuttles. Once Corbin had turned off the engine, I unbuckled, grabbed our things, and met him at the door, eager to see a planet I'd only ever heard about. Wish was a small planet that had been terraformed into what it was now—a tropical paradise for the rich and wealthy. Although there were poorer brothels on the planet as well, most of them catered to the kind of people Corbin entertained. After Corbin had gotten the job at Asiq, we'd moved to the space station closest to it, and I'd been staring at the planet for the past few years but had never thought I'd ever actually be on it.

I was nearly bouncing on the balls of my feet as my brother opened the air lock and released the pressure in the shuttle. He was taking far too much time, and I wanted to see everything. But seeing it all meant I nearly fell on my face the moment the hatch was opened, since I wasn't paying attention to the ground below me. My brother's steady hand on my shoulder stopped me, though, and I shot him a sheepish smile as he brushed himself off and straightened his clothing. I realized quickly I was far underdressed when Corbin removed his jacket and revealed a dark blue button-up shirt neatly tucked into black trousers. I looked down at my faded slacks and worn-out tee, and frowned.

"You look really good," I said, taking Corbin's jacket as he handed it to me.

He laughed. "I'm at work from the minute I land. I am as expensive as I look, and these people know that. If anyone has an interest in me, I have a stack of holocards in my pocket with Asiq's logo and my name on them so people know where to find me."

"You've got it all figured out," I replied, feeling largely out of place surrounded by all the color and style of the planet. I hadn't been to all that many planets and certainly none of them looked like this one, with its bright sunshine that found me no matter where I went.

"Hey, Corbin!"

I stopped and turned at the unfamiliar voice. Corbin smiled and eagerly shook the hand of the man who approached us. "Mr. Saunders, good to see you again. Back from Alerium so soon?"

The portly man beamed, and his thick black mustache lifted with the gesture. I didn't recognize him or his name but figured there were plenty of people Corbin was friends with whom I didn't know. I'd never realized my brother knew a Nafsu. They were supposedly a rare species of alien with gray skin and short knobs that ran over the sides of their heads and up their arms. I'd always wondered if they were hard like bone or soft, like extra bits of tissue that had grown in strange places.

"I am. I cut it short to see you boys again." There was a wink and a leering smile, and I had the good sense to bite my tongue before I said anything embarrassing as I realized Mr. Saunders was not my brother's friend, but rather a customer.

"I'm sure we're looking forward to seeing you as well, sir," Corbin replied easily. I looked up at him, wondering if the smile was an act or if he really did want to have sex with the gray-skinned Nafsu again. Maybe he was just looking forward to his money. Corbin had certainly never been all that good a liar growing up.

"And who is this?"

I felt the man's eyes on me and held still, breath catching as I felt undressed and exposed by the other man. For the first time in my life, I knew I was being objectified, and it made me feel sick. I didn't understand how my brother put up with it.

"My little brother, Thierry," Corbin said, throwing an arm around my shoulders. "He's coming to visit for the next two weeks."

I wasn't sure what the look in the man's eyes meant, but suddenly I wished I'd never agreed to come on this trip. Still, I was there, and I couldn't exactly leave now, so I figured I might have to make the best of it. I met the man's gaze for as long as I could before dropping it in a moment of shyness and uncertainty that wasn't in any part an act. My brother might have improved by leaps and bounds in the lying department, but I hadn't, and I was afraid of saying something inappropriate that would get him in trouble.

"Hey," I managed to get out, followed by a grunt as Corbin poked in me in the side.

Mr. Saunders stepped closer to me, and I smelled meat on his breath. Meat was a rare delicacy, one I didn't get often, and the unfamiliar scent was at once both alluring and revolting; my stomach twisted at being so close to a man I was sure had already pictured me naked and under him.

"Will he be on the menu tonight, as well?" he asked Corbin, his voice dropping.

I bit my tongue, wanting to tell him I'd never be on this man's menu or anything else, because I wasn't a dish at a restaurant to be eaten and consumed, but Corbin beat me to it, saving me from what I was sure would have been a disaster if I'd actually said any of the things I was thinking out loud to this man.

"Not yet, but maybe soon. I'm taking him to talk to Monroe, and he'll decide from there."

Mr. Saunders smiled and stepped back. "Good. I look forward to seeing you both sometime. Brothers are one of the few delicacies I have not enjoyed at the same time."

I suppressed my gag as Corbin poked me again as if he was giving me a preemptive warning about screwing up.

"Of course. I'll see what Monroe can do for you. I'll be dancing tonight if you want to stop by and get a drink," Corbin said with a bright smile. He touched the man's hand, and Mr. Saunders gave him a heated look as he laced his fingers with Corbin's.

"I intend to be there. You save me a seat, Corbin. I like to sit up front."

His smile grew as Corbin pulled back. "I'll make sure of it, and there will be a bottle of the best wine in the sector waiting for you, as well."

"You know how to treat a man well, boy. No wonder you're so expensive." Mr. Saunders chuckled as he turned away, and I pursed my lips to keep from saying what I was thinking until the crowd had swallowed the gray man as easily as it had released him.

"What—"

"Not here," Corbin quickly cut me off.

I wanted to argue, but the look my brother gave me killed the words on my tongue. So instead I waited and kept my mouth shut, questions swirling in my mind until Corbin pulled me through the doors of a club and farther into the building until he pushed me into a small, dark alcove away from a barrage of faces I'd barely caught glimpses of when we'd entered.

"That is a customer," Corbin hissed under his breath. "One of the best Asiq has. You can't insult him!"

"I didn't," I grumbled, pushing away from him. I moved into the hallway where I could breathe better. There were voices nearby, so I made sure to keep mine low. "Did he really mean…. Would you?" I cringed, definitely sure I was never going to do that.

Corbin snorted and leaned against the wall across from me as he stuck his hands into his pockets. "Yeah, no. But that's my point. Even if I was never going to do that with him, I can't very well say that. Do you get it?"

I imagined that yeah, I probably did. But I didn't have to like it. "Sure," I mumbled.

"Ah. There you are."

CAITLIN RICCI was fortunate growing up to be surrounded by family and teachers who encouraged her love of reading. She has always been a voracious reader and that love of the written word easily morphed into a passion for writing. If she isn't writing, she can usually be found studying as she works toward her counseling degree. She comes from a military family, and the men and women of the armed forces are close to her heart. She also enjoys gardening, hiking, and horseback riding in the Colorado Rockies she calls home with her wonderful fiancé and their two dogs. Her belief that there is no one true path to happily ever after runs deeply through all of her stories.

Website: www.CaitlinRicci.com

Prince Jai, a merciless vampire warlord, has taken up a crusade to stop the enslavement of the humans and werewolves by his own kind. He's heard tales of the time before a comet came and changed the world, and though they may just be stories told by an old human woman, he finds hope in them. After months of killing the other vampires, he's nearing his goal of taking the king's throne for himself. It's the only way to bring peace to everyone, and he won't stop until he sees that happen.

However, his men are tired, and when one clan proves to be too much for him, he agrees to a temporary peace treaty. To sweeten the deal, Jai is given the use of a blood slave, Ash. Jai detests the use of blood slaves and wants nothing to do with them. But when he realizes Ash could be another weapon in his arsenal, he spends the months training him to be everything his master has ever feared.

www.dreamspinnerpress.com

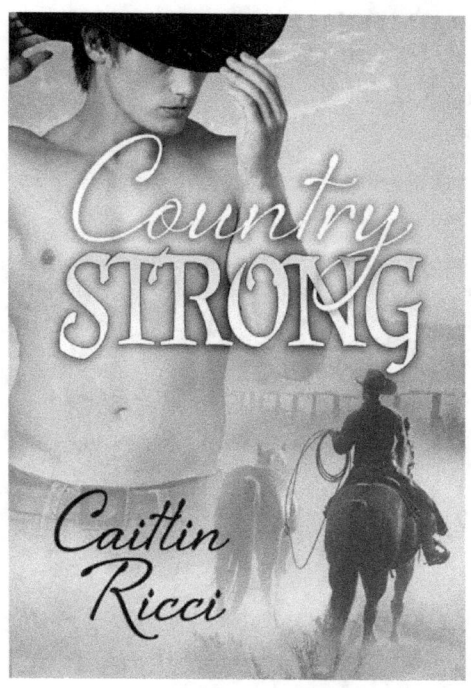

With only three months left on a lease-to-own agreement on a quarter horse Wyatt's worked hard to own, a thunderstorm spooks General and he throws Wyatt, changing both their lives forever. Luckily, Kellen, a friend of the stable owner, calls for emergency medical attention, and Wyatt comes out of the hospital with a broken wrist and a concussion.

When Wyatt returns to the stable, he finds the owner has sold General to Kellen for retraining. But Wyatt's woes have just begun, and now he must drive an hour to see his horse. The perks help balance the hardships, however, and Wyatt finds himself falling for Kellen. His fortitude is soon tested again by the ultimate betrayal when he learns Kellen doesn't intend to return General after he's trained.

www.dreamspinnerpress.com

For the Asking

CAITLIN RICCI

College student Milo Brickman is in a bind as he tries to figure out how he's supposed to afford a master's degree. His best friend points him to an ad looking for guys to star in light kink scenes. It's good money and his friend has worked for the company before, so Milo gives it a shot. On the job, Milo meets porn veteran Sullivan Craine, who Milo falls for—hard.

When Milo and Sullivan are thrown together for a scene all about denying Milo pleasure, Milo is desperate for more by the time the director yells, "Wrap!" Convincing Sullivan he's okay with a boyfriend who is not only much older than him, but who's made a career in porn, is a tough sell—but one that Milo is determined to make.

www.dreamspinnerpress.com

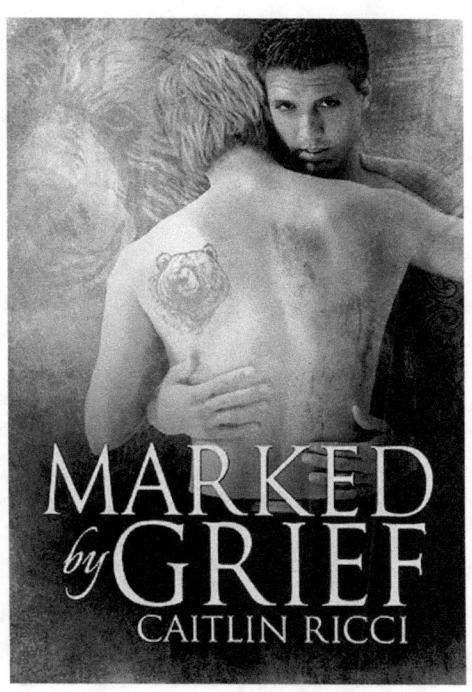

MARKED
by GRIEF
CAITLIN RICCI

Six months after Kit lost his big brother to a drunk driver, he's alone and feeling like everyone has left him behind. He struggles to get out of bed, to feed himself, to talk to his parents. Worst of all, the man he loves, his brother's best friend, hasn't spoken to him since the funeral.

Tattoo artist Jason always planned to wait until Kit was a bit more experienced and mature before he told Kit how he felt about him. But Bear's death changes everything, and Jason opts to give Kit space to heal.

However, the next time they meet, Jason is startled at how far Kit has deteriorated, so he takes him home. Simply taking care of Kit isn't enough. Marking Kit with the tattoo he demands opens a window, but Jason still isn't getting through, until he begins ordering Kit around and sees how receptive Kit is to his strong hand.

www.dreamspinnerpress.com

SEQUEL TO
RESCUING JACK

A *Forever Home*
BOOK TWO

OF
Monsters
AND *Men*

CAITLIN RICCI

A Forever Home: Book Two

Seth's life looks idyllic on the surface. He has a great job at the pet rescue with a fantastic boss, who happens to be a werewolf. He is getting his degree at the local university and has a best friend who understands that the most intimate thing for Seth is a kiss. But when it comes to relationships, Seth's perfect life is a jumbled mess. No guy stays around because eventually, they always want more than Seth, who is asexual, is able to give. Seth wants love and a relationship, but not the sex that everyone puts so much value on.

Seth tries for something more with the man he has a crush on, but when that ends Seth feels like he's back to square one. So when his boss's brother, Jeremy, pushes his way into Seth's life, insisting that he won't press for more than Seth is comfortable sharing, Seth is wary. All of Seth's experience says it won't last long. But Jeremy is one werewolf who is used to getting his way, and might just be patient enough to wait for Seth to see he means what he says.

www.dreamspinnerpress.com

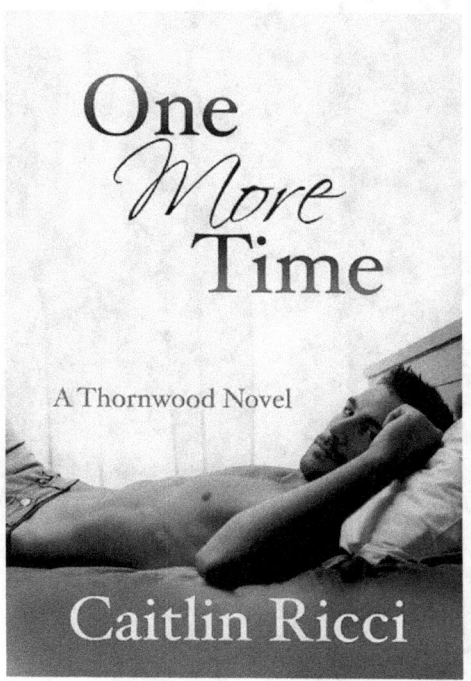

One More Time

A Thornwood Novel

Caitlin Ricci

A Thornwood Novel

Wanting to start over after breaking off a relationship with his married boss, Caleb Robinson is happy to move from Los Angeles to Thornwood, Colorado. He can barely find the town on a map, which is just the kind of place Caleb needs. He's not looking for a relationship, and Thornwood looks to be the perfect place to get lost in his art. But when Thornwood's local police officer, Trent Williams, knocks on Caleb's front door, both men have an instant attraction to each other, and Caleb's plans for solitude might have to change.

But he soon learns that Trent is a legendary one-night-stand man for a very special reason. His boyfriend has been kept on life support for the past five years after a serious skiing accident. Even though Simon isn't expected to wake up and Trent says he's trying to get past him, he won't entertain anything that comes close to commitment. As compelling as their attraction is, Caleb doesn't want to be just another hook-up, and he won't be the other man. But Trent isn't sure he can risk the pain of losing someone else he cares about, no matter how intense the chemistry between him and Caleb.

www.dreamspinnerpress.com